Silas

ADDISON JAMES

ADDISON JAMES

To my lovely readers, who never fail to make me smile—thank you.

CONTENTS

A Note From The Author

Silas takes place about two centuries before Callum, shortly before Marielle is taken captive. This is Silas and Theo's story.

Silas and Theo had a minor role in *Callum*, but there's always been more to their story. A much younger Marielle makes an appearance here, but she is not the focus of this story.

While Silas and Theo's story ties into the larger world of the Crae siblings, this book can be read on its own, if you wish.

Content Notes:
- *Magical enslavement
- *Captivity
- *Beatings and wounds from beatings
- *Blood-drinking (vampires)
- *Violence
- *On page explicit sexual content

Chapter One

Silas

Deidre's condition is getting worse.

I hear the whispers whipping through our circles. How embarrassing, a princess of the realm getting tainted blood. Never mind how it actually happened, or that it could happen to anyone. Deidre is suddenly the social pariah, and no one intends to help her.

I've waited long enough for my father to do anything about it. I assumed, apparently naively, that the people talking like they are would spur him to action. Not for any love for Deidre, of course. No man who has forty-seven children truly loves them. But I thought he would want to quash the rumors. Deirdre is his daughter, after all; surely it reflects poorly on him if people say such things. And Deidre has done so much for him that he should feel compelled to care for her.

Him not acting shouldn't be as surprising as I find it.

So I have to save my sister. There are forty-five other siblings who could step in, but none of them lift a finger for us.

I do my research. All the books I can find say that a specific concoction involving blood wart has the best chance of saving my sister. But it's not a simple concoction, and the process of stewing it can determine whether it helps her or kills her outright.

Vampires. We're immortal, lethal, and absolutely, unquestionably the kings of the world. But we live or die on the blood we consume.

There's a druid who, rumor has it, can sell me what I need if I have enough to pay for it. I might not have vast collections of wealth and land like my older brothers, but I have more than enough. I can scrounge up a payment for this druid. So, with my pockets weighted down with gems, I endure the tediously long carriage ride to his manor home.

The flowering gardens look particularly lovely, even with the sun long since set. My father has gardeners who can do that, of course, but I've found very few people bother. My opinion of the druid rises ever so slightly.

The ornate front door is carved with even more blossoming flowers, and I rap smartly on it, trying to keep myself looking calm and in control.

After a long moment, a stooped-back man opens the door. "I'm looking for the druid," I tell him.

"You've found him."

I blink, carefully looking over the man in his night clothes. He doesn't cut an especially intimidating picture. "The druid Rowan."

"Yes."

Well, then. I'm not here to quibble about the details. "I've been told that you might be able to help me."

His eyes narrow. "It's three in the morning. Come back during business hours."

"You'll find that I can't really do that," I say, then pull my lip back so he can hopefully catch on to what I mean. "Sunlight doesn't tend to agree with me."

He blinks for a moment, and I can practically hear his brain trying to process the new information.

I prompt him along. "So, the sale?"

"Come in," he mutters, stepping aside. "But keep your voice down. My household is asleep."

I wonder what exactly about my presence or demeanor indicates to him that I'm ever loud, but I let the comment pass. I still need his help, after all.

I withdraw the page of meticulously copied notes I took and hand it to him. "Can you create this?"

His eyes scan the page rapidly, taking it in. "For you?" he asks.

I bristle. Like I would ever disclose a weakness to him. "Can you make it?" I repeat. Just to make my point very clear, I reach into my pocket and produce one of the gems I'm carrying. It's a small one, but it'll hopefully make him see how serious I am about this.

His greedy eyes latch onto it, but he fakes a disdainful sniff. "It'll cost you more than that."

"I'm aware."

"Then let's get started." Then, as if he didn't just scold me and tell me to keep my voice down, he practically bellows, "Theo!"

I flinch. Surely nothing in this household needs volume that loud to hear?

A messy-haired human pokes his head over the balcony to the second floor, and then quickly trots down the stairs without saying a word.

He's a human, and a young one, too. Not a child, but not very long into his short life. "I thought you said your household was asleep," I say, looking the newcomer over.

Rowan waves a dismissive hand. "Theo hardly counts as part of the household. More part of the furniture. Isn't that right, boy?"

The boy swallows painfully, and I see a deep flash of rage in his eyes before it's quashed. "That's right, sir."

Humans who find out about us are often awed, but this is a different sort altogether. "What did you do to him?" I ask, still studying him.

Rowan waves it away. "Magic can do so much. "Now. To business?"

"To business," I agree, because yes, a timely reminder that I'm here for Deidre is necessary. But I can't turn my attention fully to Rowan.

I shouldn't care about some human. I'm not without compassion, but Deidre is the closest family I have, and I can't fathom why I'm too busy looking at the human to fully focus on the man who can save my sister.

"Theo, our visitor requires a complicated little brew. Go harvest the ingredients."

"I'm coming," I say. It's impulsive, but it feels right.

"That's not necessary."

I tear my eyes away from the human to give Rowan my best withering glare. "I'm sure you've concluded that this little concoction is only necessary when a vampire consumes tainted blood. What on earth makes you think that I won't watch every stage of every ingredient that goes into it?"

There, that sounds convincing. And it is a good reason; I should have thought of this before. But I confess it's not my only reason.

Rowan just raises an eyebrow. "Would you like me to grow the plants in front of your eyes? I warn you, the time involved would make your stay quite long. And it would involve a fair amount of sunlight."

The human shifts from foot to foot. Even humans who don't know who we are and what we can do get agitated when exposed to us. I can't imagine what a vulnerable human who knows full well what kind of damage we can do would be feeling.

"Are you saying I need to watch the process to ensure it's safe?" I ask, deceptively calm.

He scowls. "I will provide you what you're paying for." He turns to his human. "Theo, take Mister..." He trails off.

"Emrick," I supply, hoping he knows enough to know what that name means. We're not a family he should try to deceive.

He pales. "Take Mister Emrick with you. Let him watch."

Theo just nods, then quickly turns away.

I expect him to be nervous to be alone with me, a strange vampire, but if anything he relaxes as soon as we're out of Rowan's sight. Perhaps he just doesn't understand what I am.

"Are you an apprentice?" I ask as I follow him to a darkened greenhouse. I can't fathom a human apprentice, but there are human herbalists, and maybe this one decided he could learn from a druid like Rowan.

"No." He doesn't offer anything further, just starts groping around, and I realize the poor human can't even see in the dark.

"Tell me what you're looking for and I'll get it for you," I tell him.

"There's a candle somewhere."

I locate it and light it, holding it so Theo can see and still do his work. "Satisfactory?"

"Thank you."

"After you." I step back, letting him walk forward.

He gives me a hesitant look, clearly not wanting me at his back, but he doesn't protest. Because he doesn't want to, or he can't?

I suppose human servants aren't entirely unusual, given that they're so plentiful and so often desperate for money, but I don't think I know anyone who would trust their human servant to handle a tricky magical concoction on their own in the middle of the night. Humans sweep floors, tend fires, and, in households where the occupants eat, cook meals. They don't do what we can.

Theo comes to a stop by a flowering plant that matches my illustrations and fumbles around for shears. "How much?"

"Shouldn't you know?" I ask, because he's the expert here.

He huffs. "Fine. I'll guess then." Before I can give him what I learned in my research, he shoves his entire hand into the plant, and I smell the blood before he can even feel the pain.

CHAPTER TWO

SILAS

"Fuck," he hisses, withdrawing his hand and raising it, no doubt to bring to his mouth and suck the blood away.

Fortunately, I'm faster than any human, and I catch his wrist before he can take away that delicious-smelling blood. I'm much gentler than I've ever been before, but there's something precious here that I can't risk harming.

This human, this perfect human, with blood so sweet that I'm drawn in like a moth to a flame. I know what that means.

All blood smells roughly the same to me. Physical things might change it, like illness or alcohol, but the variation is smaller than non-vampires expect. Sweet blood means only one thing.

"Hey, what are you—" He tries to pull out of my grip, and I tug back gently. I don't want to tighten my hold on him and risk breaking his delicate wrist, but I won't let him go.

"Shh," I say absently, looking up at his face and away from the blood. His eyes show his fear, but also his determination. This human knows he's fragile, but he refuses to back down. I find my respect for him only growing. "Let me look at it."

He stops moving when I give the order, holding still for me while I examine the cuts. They're not too deep, and the flesh isn't torn badly enough to leave a mark later. Still, he is bleeding, and the few drops of red blood tempt me.

He tries to draw his hand back again. "Aren't you worried about tainted blood or something?"

I'm surprised he picked up on that, given he's been trying to give the impression that he doesn't know what's going on, but I don't let my surprise show. "Your blood isn't tainted," I say calmly.

He barks a short, sharp laugh. "You have any idea what he's done to me? My blood has got to be as messed up as everything else about me is."

My chest tightens in anger to hear anyone describe Theo as messed up, even Theo himself. I'll have to dissuade him of that notion. "Your blood is fine. Relax. I'm not going to hurt you." It's true, too. I've told prey that before and not meant it, but I wouldn't lie now. May my tongue wither up and fall from my mouth first.

Not interested in hearing any more protest, I bring his hand the rest of the way to my mouth and lick at the drops of blood.

The taste is divine, better than any blood I've ever had. "What are you doing to me?" he asks, his voice slurring slightly. He sounds like a man who's had too much blood taken from him, but I haven't sucked a drop out of him. He's high on pleasure.

I can't resist pressing a kiss to his palm, then reluctantly lower his hand. "Theo, I think we need to sit down and talk, because you're coming home with me tonight."

He flinches with revulsion, and my heart clenches. "You think my life isn't bad enough? You think you can buy me off Rowan and, what, suck my blood dry?"

I raise an eyebrow, trying desperately to process all the things he just said. "You think I want to kill you, Theo? Have I hurt you yet?" He looks down pointedly at his hand, and I click my tongue. "I didn't hurt you, Theo."

"You want my blood."

"I want my mate," I tell him as patiently as I can. "We don't harm our mate, Theo." I finish, considering what he's saying. "Are you afraid of Rowan?"

"Afraid?" he asks, voice strangled. He tries to take a step back again, but I'm still holding his hand. I worry his fear will make him tug hard enough to hurt himself, but I also worry that if I let him go, then I'll never see him again. "Of course I'm afraid! How do you feel when someone holds your entire life in their hands? If he told me to kill myself tomorrow, I'd have to do it, and I can never forget that."

The words *kill myself* coming out of Theo's mouth nearly set me into a frenzy, and it takes some deep breathing, laced with Theo's sweet blood, to calm myself.

I don't understand what's going on, but I need to learn quickly. I'm walking out of here tonight with my mate and the concoction I need to save my sister, and nothing will get in my way.

"What do you mean, he could tell you to kill yourself?" I demand. When he flinches again, I soften my tone. "Who is Rowan to you, Theo?"

He takes a shaky breath, and I can see the fear in his eyes illuminated by the candlelight. "Rowan bought me," he whispers. "Six or seven years ago."

Bought him? I resist baring my teeth; I don't want Theo to think I'm mad at him. "I'll take you away."

He immediately shakes his head. "No, you don't get it—there's some sort of spell. I have to listen to him. I can't leave him. He wasn't lying when he said I was like the furniture."

"A druid couldn't—" I begin, but he shakes his head again.

"I told you, he bought me. From someone else. I don't know—I didn't know any of this was real, alright, until it happened. And you probably think that's funny—Rowan certainly enjoys surprising me—but that's the truth. Someone else took me, and they did this to me, and then Rowan paid him and now I'm here."

I open my mouth to try to ask more questions. I need to know what type of magic it is, how Rowan's control works, and how I can help Theo out of it. But I don't get my chance to ask, because stomping footsteps pierce the air.

"What the fuck is taking so long?" Rowan demands, grumpily storming into the greenhouse.

I straighten up, dropping Theo's hand. I need to think quickly to avoid getting him in any trouble. "You sent a human to do a druid's job," I say, trying to muster the icy coolness that comes so easily when handling my siblings. "He injured himself. His blood was tempting."

A dark look crosses Rowan's face. "You better not have damaged him permanently. He's valuable."

"No permanent damage," I say dismissively. "Just a taste."

Rowan looks me over for a moment, and I refuse to break. He finally looks at Theo. "Get the damn cuttings, boy."

I want to protest on his behalf—Theo is mine, and members of my household don't take orders from bottom-feeders like Rowan. But I don't understand what kind of compulsion Theo is under, so I don't say anything. Better for me to understand things before I go wading in.

***

Rowan doesn't leave us alone for the entire rest of the time it takes him to brew my cure for Deidre, and by the time he's done, the sun is dangerously close to rising. I pocket the little concoction, handing over the gems in my pocket. "I'll be back, most likely," I say, trying to project cool disinterest while simultaneously staring a hole in Theo, willing him to get my message. "A partnership between you and my kind might be productive."

Rowan is too busy staring at the gems I handed him to notice anything suspicious in my tone, and I get one last long look at Theo before the door is closed in my face.

CHAPTER THREE

THEO

Marielle wakes me in the morning, her eyes wide and her hand over my mouth. It's unnecessary; I know better than to make sounds when I could be heard by now.

"I covered for you for as long as I could," she whispers. "But he'll call for you soon."

And it's much kinder to be woken up by Marielle than pulled from a dead sleep by the rope of my name dragging me by the heart back to Rowan.

I nod, and she releases my mouth and lets me sit up. "How is he?" I whisper.

She shrugs, eyes darting around like she expects him to appear out of thin air to hear her. Marielle is terrified of her father, despite the fact that I've never seen him physically hurt her. "Something happened last night," she says instead of answering.

I swallow. Not a strange dream, then. I don't know why I thought it would be—I haven't dreamed in years, like Rowan took those away from me too—but a vampire who shows up and licks my hand before declaring he wants to take care of me and take me from here feels like it couldn't be anything but a dream.

"A wealthy client showed up," I tell her instead of explaining.

She nods. "That makes sense. He seems lighter. He said thank you this morning."

If my heart belonged to me, it would break. She's so young and still gets excited when he's nice to her, but she's jaded enough that she tries not to. She knows he's never going to love her, but she can't help but hope.

Marielle shouldn't be someone I care about. She's privileged in this world, and she's never been hungry and never been beaten. She has a power in her that can't be taken away, and on my worst days, where Rowan really beats me down, I can't help but resent her a bit.

But truthfully, I can't hate her. I like her. Marielle was nine years old when I met her, and she's never understood why someone else should do a task that she can complete. She's always working by my side whenever Rowan isn't paying attention.

And she goes beyond that, too. Like this morning when she let me sleep, she'll cover for me as much as she can. She ensures I have enough to eat on a regular basis. She'll try to talk her father out of hurting me, although she's rarely successful.

Hell, she taught me to read. When she was younger, she'd find me after her lessons and, like a little domineering lady, insist on teaching them to me, and I'd let her because she'd pick up work right beside me as she did. I learned to read, and while I doubt I'll ever have the opportunity to use that skill to better myself in the world, it still feels good.

There's a tug in my chest, and I curse. "He's looking for me," I whisper.

Her eyes go wide. "I can try to distract him?"

"No need." Rowan doesn't much care about his daughter, so she struggles to distract him without acting out in some way, and I want her to do that sparingly. "I can go do whatever he needs."

"You look tired, Theo," she whispers as I'm already standing.

I always look tired. I don't remember not being tired anymore. I don't say that to her, though. What can she do? "I'll be alright," I assure her, then I leave the cupboard we call my bedroom, and unerringly go straight to Rowan.

***

The best I can describe the magic is that it's a rope. Rowan tugs on his end by saying my name, and I'm compelled to do whatever he asks. If I don't, then it hurts. It doesn't work on anyone else. Marielle isn't a demanding person, but even if she was, she could never compel me the way her father does. Clients of Rowan's can demand things of me, and I'll do them because I know Rowan will be angry if I don't, but I'm not mystically forced to.

I don't remember my life before the spell. I wonder sometimes if that's a blessing or a curse, and who I might have left behind. Does my mother mourn me? I think I was too young to be married, but did I leave a sweetheart?

I don't remember them, and I hope for their sake that they forgot about me long ago. It's not like I'll be coming back.

No, I have no doubt I'll die here. I've never quite had the courage to ask Marielle if there was someone before me. The information won't help me; I can't escape my fate whether or not she knows what will happen to me.

Marielle is going to live forever, something I can't quite wrap my mind around. She's still a child, sixteen years old, and she's still growing. But someday, she'll be fully grown and immortal, and I'll be dead and probably buried somewhere on this property while she's still walking around. I wonder if she'll be as nice to whoever her father enslaves next.

Except she probably won't still be here. Rowan hasn't been shy about his plans to marry her off to whoever pays well for her. So I'll be buried, and

Marielle will live forever with whatever terrible person her father gives her to, and she'll forget me.

I can't stop thinking about this when I sweep up the mess Rowan left around his work station. I try not to think about these things—it doesn't help—but today I can't get them out of my head. That, paired with the memory of the intense stare from that vampire, and I'm completely unaware of my surroundings when Rowan walks back in.

"You're not done yet?" he barks, and I nearly drop the broom. I'm usually more alert than this, usually do better; I can't afford not to be more alert.

"Almost," I croak out.

"The back garden needs weeding."

I bite my lip so I don't say that I'm pretty sure he can garden with magic in seconds what will take me all afternoon. Marielle probably could too, but she'll at least come help me with the task if she can get away.

"I'll go there next."

"Move faster." He turns to walk away, having no need to stay to make sure his order is obeyed, but then stops. "Last night."

I freeze. Last night still feels like a strange dream. "Yes?"

"That vampire. Emrick. He didn't hurt you?"

Like he cares if I get hurt. No, he just wants to make sure his property wasn't irrevocably damaged. "No."

"Good." Then he turns to leave, and I finish sweeping quickly, the compulsion to get to the garden nearly overwhelming.

Chapter Four

Silas

My driver brings the carriage straight through the front gates to get me inside and out of the sun. All vampire dwellings are built this way, with too-large entries for just this purpose.

Deidre waits for me at the bottom of the grand staircase. Her eyes latch onto me, even if I can still see the sickness burning behind them. "Do you have it?"

I've been clutching the little concoction in my pocket the entire way home, worrying at it with my thumb. I did indeed get her what she needs, and the cost of it was leaving my mate behind.

I'll go back for him. I don't know how yet, but of course I will. I'll take him from there, and I won't make him wait long.

I don't fully understand why he's there, so I need to get him alone to ask some questions, which is easier said than done when Rowan is stomping around. But I'll find a way. I always do.

Case in point, everyone has written Deidre off for dead. They've dismissed a painful and lingering death as the consequences of her own choices, and turned their backs. But not me. No, I've found a way to cure her.

I hand her the little bottle. "Try this," I instruct. "Wait a day. Then tell me how you are."

She snatches it out of my hand so fast that I feel a breeze as she moves. Before I can say anything else, she pulls out the stopper and drinks the entire thing, making a face as she does. "It doesn't taste good."

"It's not supposed to. And when was the last time you drank anything but blood?"

She shrugs. "Sometimes liquor can be a nice change of pace."

"This isn't some drink at a party, Deidre. It's medicinal. It's meant to cure you." I take a breath to reset myself. Deidre fully knows what's happened to her, and she doesn't need a lecture. "It should start to work within the hour," I tell her gently. "Take it easy today, rest if you can. By tomorrow, you should be better."

"And where will you be going?" she demands, clearly able to tell I'm barely restraining myself from getting straight back into the carriage.

"I found someone," I say vaguely. "And I need to investigate."

I've learned over the years not to say too much until I have a more secure grip on the situation. Deidre is my closest sibling, and the one I trust the most in the world. If I were like my father, I'd take some faith in the fact that I just saved her life and therefore put her in my eternal debt. But even so, I won't say anything until I'm ready.

Deidre's eyes light up. "My type of investigating?" she asks.

Deidre knows how to get information from people. Deidre can read people as well as I can read books, and she always knows just what to say to get them to tell her every secret they've hidden away for decades. What other people see as a wild party, Deidre sees as a fertile hunting ground, and she pretends to be the wild child of the family while funneling so many secrets back to our father.

"Not your type of investigating," I tell her stiffly, because the idea of Deidre plying Theo with alcohol and flirtatious comments makes me sick. "And you are in no condition to go investigate anything."

Her last party got a tad out of hand, and Deidre ended up sick. From what I understand, at least the courtier who'd served her tainted blood had also consumed it, and I'm not going out of my way to spare him.

Deidre hoists up the empty little bottle like it's a champagne flute. "Perhaps not, but give me a day," she says, smiling. She's lost weight, looking gaunt from the pain and illness. I know she'll put the weight back on as soon as she recovers, but right now it makes her smile look skeletal. "And then I can investigate whatever you wish."

"Not that type of investigation," I remind her, and then leave to make plans.

***

I wait until nearly dusk, entering the carriage under cover and drawing the curtains so I can travel in safety. The summers here are the worst, and daylight is an aberration. I know there are places with much longer stretches of daylight than here, and I can't imagine ever living there. I suppose I spend enough of my time inside, rifling through dusty libraries, that I might not notice how much the sun limits our kind for a while. But on days like today, it's intolerable.

Thankfully, the sun is fully set when I return to Rowan's mansion, leaving the comforting blanket of darkness to keep me safe as I seek out my mate. I ignore the front door entirely, walking around the side of the building, intent on finding another way in so I can avoid Rowan entirely.

I have no desire to speak to the man who apparently bought my mate like cattle, and if I have any hope of finding out the truth, I certainly can't have him involved.

I don't even have to hunt for a way in. Theo is right there in the garden, on his hands and knees, weeding. "Doesn't his magic take care of that?"

He jumps, and I feel his pulse race, his delicious blood pounding faster through his body. "What are you doing back here?" he demands.

I shrug, sliding my hands into my pockets. "Looking for you. What else?"

"Why? Decided I'd make a good meal?"

I crouch in the dirt next to him. Ruining my trousers is a low price to pay for time with my mate.

Theo flinches back as I get closer, and I take a deep breath to remind myself that this is okay. The hurt in my heart when he flinches is to be expected, but it's nothing we can't recover from. I'll help Theo, and he'll see that I'm worth considering.

Humans don't have mates. Not that Theo will be a human much longer—he'll have to be a vampire to enter my world, and then he'll feel the bond too. But right now, he's a human, and he's scared.

"I was serious when I said I'd take you with me," I tell him quietly. "Unless you like the work."

"No one likes work they're forced to do," Theo says sharply. "That doesn't mean I can go."

There has to be a way out, but I know that if I push right now, he'll shut me out. I don't think he'd alert Rowan to my presence, because I think he hates Rowan far more than me, so I don't have to worry about that at least. But he could refuse to talk to me, and that would get us nowhere.

"Then let's talk," I say, settling deeper into the dirt.

He tries to pull some more weeds, and I can't help notice his fingers shaking. Is this normal human frailty, or is it his nerves? "About what?" he asks.

I shift to start pulling weeds myself. "If you could do anything in the world, what would you do?"

"Sleep," he murmurs immediately, an undeniable deep longing in his voice. "I'd love to sleep."

"And after you slept?" I ask once I work through that answer. Such a simple answer; such a tragic answer.

He shrugs. "If I had dreams, I don't remember them. I don't have time to think about a future that will never happen."

"You don't want money? A castle? Fine wine?" I press, thinking of all the things my family has.

Theo stops pretending to weed and turns to look at me, and it feels like he can see my soul. The pain in his eyes makes me freeze. "If you think any of that is even remotely in my thoughts—I want to know I'm safe. I want to sleep. I want to make my own choices forevermore, and never be beholden to anyone. I want to have enough to eat and not wonder when I'll die."

"I can give you that," I promise. I slide forward on my knees, almost subconsciously, just needing to be closer to him. "I can give you all of that, Theo."

"Why do you even want to?"

I consider it for a moment. Why I'd want to has never factored into this for me: I want to because he's mine. But I try to put it in language he'll understand. "I was born little more than dead," I murmur. "I imagine a human mother would throw away a vampire baby, completely unaware we're even alive. My heart beats, but it beats slower than yours. I don't need to breathe except as part of a sense of smell. I can never see the sun. I need blood to live. And I was happy like that. There are things that can make a life like that worthwhile. But the truth is it's cold, and I always knew that someday, there'd be someone else. Fate decreed it so; it's the compensation for barely being alive."

Theo makes me feel alive in a way I never have before. I don't know if he can understand that, and I don't know if I can explain it. But I know that, over the course of the last day, this man has become my life blood. There is no me if there is no him.

"You don't know me," he denies, turning his head away. "You know nothing about me, and I know nothing about you, and you can't know if I'm that person to you."

I smelled his blood and knew. I tasted it and my world changed forever. There was a warmth in me that I've never felt before. I could absolutely gorge on blood, be an indolent glutton, and I could curl up in the warmest, softest down blankets, and yet I still wouldn't be half as warm as I am in his presence. It's not even just his blood, although that's certainly a part of it. But I know that telling him his blood lights up my world will just scare him away.

"What do you want to know?" I ask instead.

He turns to look at me again, and I once again get the eerie feeling that he can see everything about me. I've never wanted anyone to know me that well before—not lovers, not my siblings, not even my own mother—but I feel another rush of warmth, knowing he sees everything. I want to open myself up and let him in. I just need him to want it too.

"I don't even know your name," he says clearly, and the warmth dissipates.

I licked blood off his hand without even telling him my name. Some mate I am.

My father is not the best model for successful relationships, considering he lost his mate long, long ago and has kept what is essentially a harem ever since. But from what I've seen, on the rare occasions where he feels the need to apologize, gems and gold and fine clothes and expensive liquor seem to be what fixes his problems—all the things my mate denied wanting.

"Silas," I tell him, my voice a little hoarse. "My name is Silas."

"Silas Emrick," he muses. When most people say my last name, they sound fearful. Even as an insignificant minor son, Emrick still carries a heavy weight. But Theo doesn't know enough of the world to know that. It sounds perfectly fine, perfectly neutral, coming from him.

Am I a terrible mate for bringing him into this family? Four of my father's many wives have been assassinated over the years. The family would have left Deidre to die without a second thought. Theo doesn't have any defenses in that world.

Yes, he does, I resolve. I will be his defense until he can defend himself. I might still be selfish, but I can't stop myself. I need him, and I'll protect him.

He needs me, too. He's trapped here by some mystical nonsense I can't parse through, and I am going to give him freedom and anything else he desires.

"What else do you want to know?" I prompt, and I reach for the weeds again.

He softens when my hands sink into the dirt. "Are you a vampire?" He whispers the last word. "I guessed, when I saw..." He looks intently at my mouth.

When he saw my teeth getting close to his skin last night, no doubt. "I am," I agree. "Does that scare you?"

It's obvious from his eyes that he's scared, but I need him to voice it so I can start counteracting his fears.

He shrugs. "I've adjusted to magic and mystical nonsense," he says, turning his attention to a particularly stubborn weed. "I've had to. And I know Rowan and Marielle are tamer than some of the people who have come to buy things from Rowan, but even their magic is a lot."

"Marielle?"

"Rowan's daughter."

"Does she hurt you too?"

"She's a child," he dismisses. "And if her father wasn't so insistent on marrying her to someone who will pay money for her and therefore making her learn how to play the harpsichord right this moment, then she'd be out here weeding right alongside me."

Well, that eases something in me just the slightest bit. At least there's someone in this house who Theo likes. "What about being near a vampire scares you?"

"You drink blood."

"Correct."

"You kill humans to do that?" he asks, not looking at me still.

"Very rarely. And it doesn't have to be humans. Another vampire wouldn't give me very valuable blood, since it would have already been used up by their body, but I could even drink from them in a pinch. It could be any creature."

"Does it hurt them?"

"It can if I'm not careful," I say, because I don't want to lie to him. "But I'm almost always careful."

"Almost always?"

I shrug. "Sometimes the source of my meal might deserve a little bit of pain." Like Rowan, for instance. If I suck Rowan dry, will his spell on Theo end?

"What's so special about my blood?" he asks.

"Who said there is something special about it?"

"You did, when you looked like it was a divine revelation last night when you tasted mine."

I snort, because he's not wrong, and it's not like I expected to be able to hide my obsession with my mate. My thoughts never leave him; it's like a constant cyclone that always circles back to him. Of course I can't hide it.

"You're special," I tell him.

"You weren't that interested in me until the blood."

"Blood is life for vampires." I shrug. "We live and die by it. I don't drink blood because I like to, Theo. It's the only sustenance I've ever known. The only sustenance I ever will know. My body lives and dies by blood; yours is particularly warm and inviting."

It's an understatement, but what little I know about humans tells me that they're not interested in hearing us rhapsodize about the beauty of blood.

"What do you want with a human, if you're not just here for my blood?" he challenges me, shoulders firm like he thinks he won this argument.

"You're my mate, human or not."

"I don't drink blood, I'm fragile, and I'll die eventually," Theo lists dispassionately.

"So will I." We might live a long time, but we all die.

"I'll die soon. Maybe very soon, if things continue like they are."

"Is Rowan hurting you?" I ask sharply, latching onto the morose words.

He rolls his eyes. "You think enslavement doesn't hurt?"

"I mean in some way that would make you feel like you're dying."

"I work day in and day out. I can barely sleep. Every time he calls my name, I feel a little more apathetic and a little less sure it's even worth it to keep on living. And yes, when I don't make him happy, he's perfectly willing to beat me. Does that answer your question?"

I look down, ashamed. It was a stupid question to begin with. Theo deserves better from me than this—I have to learn.

My life might not have always been easy, but I've never had everything stripped from me like Theo has. I live in a castle, and can pursue what I want. Yes, I have enough older siblings that we couldn't all eat at the same table if we were inclined to eat, but even my most pig-headed older brothers don't interfere with my life much. I get to just be.

Theo doesn't have that luxury. "I will find a way to save you from this," I promise him. "I'm quite good at research. I'll find a way out of this for you."

"No, you won't," he says, voice dead with what I can only assume is exhaustion. "And I think it's crueler to let me believe it than to admit the truth."

Hope hurts Theo, and I suppose I can understand that. That's fine; I don't need him to believe it yet. I can believe it for both of us.

CHAPTER FIVE

THEO

He has to leave eventually, although he does help me pull weeds before he goes.

"I'll be back," he says, which is uncomfortably too close to the promises he keeps trying to make. At least he doesn't say he'll save me again.

It's long after midnight by the time I make it inside. Silas' presence slowed my work down a little, but I doubt I would have finished that much faster without him. My need for rest is never taken into account around here.

Marielle is waiting for me when I make it to the broom cupboard I call a bedroom, and she has the remnants of dinner for me. "Someone was here with you," she murmurs when I start to eat. "I saw. I didn't want to interrupt; you looked like you were talking to him."

This girl is too damn trusting. Not that I think Marielle should jump between a vampire and someone he's set his sights on, but the fact that it didn't ever occur to her to worry about someone she's never met before being around the house and talking to me is a sign of such innocence that I can barely believe it.

I wonder if Marielle could handle herself against a vampire in a fight, if it came down to it. She looks like an innocent, wealthy child, but that might work to her advantage. I know she has more magic in her than people suspect when looking at her.

Plus, she could surprise any attacker with some fast reflexes and good instincts with a knife. I started teaching her one day when we were taking cuttings in the greenhouse and she started playing with the knife. I think she'd been reading stories about brave adventurers and heroes, but her footwork and grip had been appalling. I don't know how I'd known, but I had, the same way I know how to speak or take care of basic tasks, I suppose. Some things are just instinct.

So I'd shown her how to do better, a lesson she'd demanded again and again. She could certainly surprise an attacker with a quick stab wound.

But it's a moot point, because Marielle isn't going to fight a vampire. I don't think Silas would fight her, which might be incredibly naïve of me, but I think if I say she's important to me, then he would leave her alone. Silas might be crazy to have become obsessed with me so quickly—or he's blinded by his thirst for my blood, despite him saying that the blood isn't the root of his obsession—but I do think he's genuine. He wants to make me happy.

"Someone came to see me," I confirm for Marielle, taking the plate from her hand.

Her eyes light up. "Someone you knew from before?"

She must not have gotten a good look at him, then, if she didn't realize what he is. But I'm not going to tell her. Marielle tries to avoid her father at all costs, but the information that a vampire is stalking around the property might just be the thing that sends her running to him.

It's not even the thought that Rowan would inevitably punish me that makes me bite my tongue. I try to avoid punishments, of course, but I can take them. No, what really makes me keep this to myself is the fear of losing Silas.

Silas might be crazy. He might get bored of me and never speak to me again. He might just be after my blood. Any of this could be true, but what is also true is that he's mine. He's here for me, and I haven't had something that's mine in my entire memory.

I don't even know if he'll come back, but I find myself hoping he does.

Hope. What a strange, foreign emotion.

"Not someone I knew from before," I contradict. "Someone I'm getting to know now."

Her eyes light up. "You like him."

Spoken like a child who reads too many stories with a romantic happy ending. "I like him," I agree regardless. "And Rowan..." I hesitate to say it. I don't want to put her in a difficult position.

She gets it immediately, though. Of course she does; she knows what he's like. "Rowan can't find out," she agrees. "I'll help hide him."

I set the plate aside so I can take her hand and give it a squeeze. "Thank you, Marielle," I whisper. She's a good girl.

She squeezes my hand back. "You deserve something good, Theo."

And I might be really losing the last of my sanity now, but I can't help but agree that Silas is indeed a good thing.

***

I'm cleaning the remaining dinner dishes when raised voices in the foyer catch my attention.

"So, we thought it best to build a stockpile," Silas says smoothly. "For emergency purposes."

I peek around the corner, ducking back out of sight when Rowan turns his head. Silas is dressed like some sort of foreign king, all expensive fabrics and sharp looking edges and jewelry that could probably buy this house a few times over.

Rowan is pretending not to be impressed, but I know him. The man cares about status and money. Why else would he practically be salivating to marry Marielle to someone wealthy? Honestly, Silas is probably just the type of man that Rowan wants for Marielle.

The thought hurts, which is ridiculous, because I know neither of them even knows the other exists, never mind would be interested in each other. I'm feeling hurt about something that hasn't happened and, if it did happen, would be out of their control.

Well, out of Marielle's control, anyway. Silas doesn't strike me as the kind of person who lets anyone dictate his choices, and that makes me feel a little better.

"You understand that will cost you a small fortune?" Rowan asks him.

"Are you insinuating that vampires can't pay?" Silas' voice sounds pleasant enough, but there's a low undercurrent of threat.

Rowan's silence is an answer. "Alright, then."

"And I want your lovely assistant," Silas adds blithely.

"What?"

"You heard me. He's interesting."

"You want to eat him." Rowan's voice is flat when he says it, and I shouldn't be surprised by the total lack of care for me. Whether or not Silas would actually hurt me is irrelevant; Rowan thinks he will and doesn't care.

And then Rowan surprises me by saying, "No." I jolt in surprise, nearly knocking into the ornate vase by the door, but then Rowan says, "Do you have any idea how much I've invested in him? Letting you drain him would be akin to robbing me blind."

"Then let me buy him off of you," Silas says, still maintaining the same barely interested tone. "You know I can afford it."

"Was his blood so good that you'd piss away money for another chance?" Rowan actually laughs just thinking about that, like the idea that I could be worth something to someone is ludicrous. "Anyways, you can't. The way the spell works, he won't survive separation from me."

I won't survive being around him much longer, either. I feel it, the lethargy, the emptiness inside. There's not a lot of *me* left.

I probably would have just given up and died years ago if it weren't for Marielle. She at least makes me want to live another few days.

And now, with Silas here—I haven't truly let myself think about leaving, because it hasn't felt real. But I have to admit that I feel a stab of disappointment at hearing what I've long suspected.

I'm here until I die. It's not a question of if, just a question of when.

"That's some spell," Silas says, his voice carefully neutral.

"It's useful to have someone around whose loyalty you never question," Rowan says, and I have to grit my teeth. It's unfortunately true, because I simply can't work against him. But loyal is the exact opposite of how I feel. If Marielle didn't live in this house, I know I'd find a way to burn it down with Rowan and I both inside it.

"I suppose so," Silas agrees. "Any chance I can get a taste of him either way?"

Rowan is silent for a long moment. "Can you do that without harming him?"

"If we killed every human we fed from, then we'd have killed off all the humans. I can keep him alive perfectly fine."

"Perhaps we can negotiate," Rowan says.

I shouldn't be surprised that Rowan would so easily sell me. And, given the circumstances, I'm not angry. I much rather be alone with Silas than with Rowan. But the fact that he'd sell me—that he doesn't even put up a cursory protection of me—well, that somehow still stings.

Silas hands Rowan more gems, not even counting them. "Shall we begin?"

Rowan sniffs. "Just because you want a taste doesn't mean the boy can neglect his duties. I trust you remember where the greenhouse is?"

Chapter Six

Silas

Rowan is actually stupid enough to leave me alone with my mate.

I smile at Theo, nodding to let him know we're alone. I can hear Rowan moving around somewhere, presumably hiding away the payment I just handed him. There's someone else in the house too, young with light, quick steps, but I pay them no mind. It's the girl Theo mentioned, and as long as she doesn't interfere, then I don't need to worry about her.

"If I didn't think it'd hurt you, I'd tear him apart," I tell him, flashing my teeth as I do so. I mean it, too. Rowan is nothing to me, and he's prey that would be easily forgotten if his fate didn't affect Theo's.

"Keep your voice down."

"He can't hear us right now. Don't worry, darling. I'll keep an eye out for us."

His head jerks to look at me when I call him darling, and I fight a smirk. So he likes that. Well, good. I like calling him that.

"Why do you want so much of this?" he grumbles instead of acknowledging what I said, picking up over-sized shears so he can cut some of the plant that cut his hand open last time.

"Let me, darling," I say, pleased when he reacts the same this time that he did last time. "Wouldn't want you to cut your hand again."

"I was under the impression that you liked my blood."

"Not enough to want you to hurt over it. No, if you want to give me blood, please just tell me. I'll make you feel wonderful."

"You'll tear open my skin... and it'll feel wonderful?" he asks skeptically.

"Orgasmic," I pronounce, watching him flush as he processes the word.

"Silas," he hisses.

It turns out that I like hearing him say my name as much as he likes being called darling. But now isn't the time to reflect on that, so I busy myself cutting small clippings for Theo to hand over to Rowan. "To answer your question, I don't really need more of what Rowan's making me, but I suppose it's handy enough to have around."

"And expensive."

"Cost doesn't affect me. The gems I paid with? I could find those between the sofa cushions." It's not bragging if it's true, and a part of me wants Theo to know I can offer him so much more than anything he's ever had before.

Not that that's saying much. I could offer him a spot in my stable and some peace and quiet and regular meals and he'd be content. But I can do so much better. I can show him what he deserves.

"Must be nice," Theo murmurs, looking at the pile of clippings I'm cutting.

"It's yours now, too." I wait for him to tell me to stop, but he doesn't, so I keep cutting.

"I can hardly carry jewels around here."

"You're right. Carry them around in my home." Or wear them. The image of Theo wearing nothing but jewels is too tempting.

"I'd have to be able to leave. And you heard Rowan; that's not happening. I'm stuck with him."

"Do you know anything about the spell he used?" I ask, trying to piece this together. Every instinct in me tells me to get my mate out of this place as soon as possible. If I leave him here, then I've failed him.

Theo is quiet for a moment, but then he whispers, "When he first took me, he showed me a document. He said it was my spell, and that it meant he owned me. He proved it, too, ordering me to do all sorts of ridiculous shit until it really sank in. And then he locked that paper in his safe." He huffs. "But I couldn't read then, so he could have been lying to me I suppose."

He wasn't lying, though. Someone like Rowan would have loved to rub that type of power in Theo's face, while simultaneously believing Theo could never be a threat to him. He absolutely would have shown him the spell.

"Fire breaks a lot of spells," I muse. "It's cleansing, in a way. If you could get to that document and burn it…"

"How am I supposed to get to it? Stop cutting."

It takes me a second to process the order, and when I do my hand slips, allowing the thorns I've been so carefully avoiding to tear the back of my hand. "Fucker."

"Let me see," Theo says instantly, already holding out his own hand for mine, and my heart warms. It's an unnecessary gesture, of course, because my hand is already healed by the time he raises it for a look, shallow scratches completely healed and only a few lonely drops of blood left behind.

Theo stares at the droplets. "They're darker."

"When our body processes the nutrients in the blood, it changes the blood slightly. It's different from yours now—only the useless bits left." I smile at him, trying to be charming as he continues to hold my hand. "Did you want a taste, Theo?"

"Gross."

"Don't say that until you try it," I tease, then gently extract my hand. "Would that girl help you? Is she really better than her father?"

"I don't want him to hurt her," Theo says instantly.

My mate is kind, I realize slowly, a rarity in my world.

"If she really cares, if she really is better than Rowan, she'd do it," I tell him. I should engineer a situation to meet the girl, but that might draw too much attention from Rowan. Still, I think she could be a useful tool in freeing my mate.

"I'll ask her," he says grudgingly. He doesn't look me in the eye, though. "When will I see you again?"

I smile, then check where Rowan is. Still far away. I lean in and kiss his cheek, being incredibly daring. He doesn't move away, but he does stop breathing for a moment. "I'll never be too far, darling. That's a promise."

CHAPTER SEVEN

THEO

He's infuriating. I'll never be too far? That's not an answer to my question, and now I can't help but feel like he's watching me, even when I'm all the way inside the house and locked in my little cupboard.

Marielle finds me late in the evening, ink smudged across her nose and curls an untamed mess, which tells me she hasn't seen Rowan in hours. He'd have something to say about her appearance.

I should ask her. Silas isn't wrong that she'd want to help, and she's more likely to be successful than I am. But she's a child, and just as vulnerable to harm as I am. Rowan could seriously hurt her if he's mad enough. Not to mention, if he really keeps valuable things in his safe, he could have laid any number of mystical traps on it.

Marielle is probably talented enough to detect them. Probably. It's not a risk we should take.

I tell myself that firmly, but it leaves me disquieted. So I'm going to stay here forever? Ignore Silas and his too-tempting offers? I'm just going to let Rowan kill me, take all this lying down?

I don't know who I was before all this started, but I get a feeling that I never was someone to take something without a fight.

"If I distracted your father, do you think you could break into his study?" I ask her quietly. My voice is barely a whisper, like Rowan is going to suddenly pop out from under my pillow. The words hang heavy yet fragile between us, and she just blinks at me, long and slow.

"Distracted him how?" she asks, because she's clever. There's only so many things I can do that would truly distract her father.

So I don't answer. "But could you do it?"

"Do you need money, Theo?" she asks, again without answering. She leans a little closer. "What could you need money for?"

That is a fair question. I never go anywhere, never see anyone outside of this house. I certainly don't own anything. "Not money, Marielle. I think the contract that he has over me is in there."

"You think?"

"He showed it to me, but it was before you taught me how to read. So I can't know for sure. But if it is..."

"What do you need to do?" she asks, voice barely above a whisper.

"Burn it, I think." I don't mention Silas. I don't know if she'll react positively to the idea coming from someone else. If she doesn't trust Silas' word, she might back out.

"I can do that. And then you'll... leave?"

Her voice trembles, but she doesn't break eye contact. I'm struck again that I am the only person in the world who cares for this girl.

I can't stay for her. I shouldn't stay for her. I deserve to live, and I'll die here. I deserve freedom, choice. Maybe even love.

But likewise, I can't take her with me. What do I know about the vampires? Perhaps they're cruel. Perhaps they hurt young women. Perhaps Silas has told me nothing but lies. And that's a risk I can take for myself, but I won't take it for Marielle.

"I'll leave," I tell her. "And when I can, I'll come back to take you with me." Maybe it's a lie, but I hope not. I hope I can make a home for both of us.

Her eyes light up. "I'd like to live in a little human village," she murmurs, already day-dreaming about it. I don't quite have the heart to tell her that's never happening.

Marielle looks like a damn forest sprite in a fairy story. She's going to live forever. She makes plants grow with a wave of her hand, and flowers sometimes bloom in her footsteps without her even trying. The idea of her with humans—if I even had a human village to take her to—is ludicrous.

"Someday we'll both leave," I promise her instead of responding.

"But you need to leave now," she surmises.

"I do. Marielle, I'm—I'm dying. Surely you can see that too."

"I can," she says, voice barely a whisper. "I'll help you. I want you to go."

She's being brave, but I think she's being sincere too, and I don't think I've ever loved her more.

"When do you want me to do it?"

I stop and think. I can't stay here after it happens. I'll have to be able to go right away, which means Silas needs to know what's happening. Hopefully, he was being serious when he promised he'd be around.

"You'll know when," I tell her, not wanting to explain me needing Silas. But it's true regardless; I usually do everything I can to avoid being in trouble with Rowan, so she'll know the moment is right when I do it on purpose.

"Be careful," she whispers.

And then she leaves me all alone, contemplating my future.

***

I spend the next day hoping Silas will come and linger outside for as long as I can, hoping Rowan doesn't notice that I'm taking too long. After dusk, Silas appears silently beside me like he just formed out of the shadows. I study him for a second, taking in his thin, pointy face and keen eyes, his thin mouth that I know hides those oddly sharp teeth. Those eyes peer into me, and I somehow haven't ever felt better.

"You're here."

"I told you I'd come," he says, smiling and showing those fangs.

"I have a plan," I whisper, like someone is going to appear and overhear me.

"Oh?" Silas looks around. "Should we get further away?"

"I need to be able to hear Rowan if he calls—I can't have him notice anything is wrong yet." I reflexively look over my shoulder. "You don't hear him coming, do you?"

"No, not right now," he assures me. "We'll stay here. I'll keep an ear out. Tell me your plan."

I feel incredibly foolish for a minute, about to spill all the details I've put into this plan to run away with a man I barely know. But I square my shoulders and say it anyway. I need to leave whether or not Silas willingly takes me with him. Silas could abandon me tomorrow, and I'd still need to leave.

"Could you be here tomorrow night?" I ask. "Marielle is going to steal the spell and burn it. And then... I can leave." Hopefully, at least. I don't mention that part.

"I'll be here just after dark," he murmurs. "So we have more time to put distance between this place and ourselves. Does that work?"

Just after dark. I swallow, then resolve myself, nodding. Yes, I can handle that.

"Can we sit for a while?" Silas asks.

Everything in me aches to say yes, because somehow I just know he'll be comforting when I feel on the edge of falling apart. But… "Better not. Don't want Rowan to suspect."

Silas looks like he swallowed something unpleasant, but nods. "You do what you have to do protect yourself," he says. "And I'll see you tomorrow night. And every night thereafter." And he says it with so much conviction that I have to believe it too.

Chapter Eight

Silas

After a confession to my sister of where I've been and who I've found, Deidre, myself, and our servants prepare the home for my soon-to-arrive guest. The home is kept in good condition, but I'm pushing for a level of perfection that is probably not truly obtainable. I need to impress my mate.

I don't stop until Deidre asks me, "One bedroom or two?"

Our father has his own bedroom in his home, and his harem of mistresses stays elsewhere, coming to him when he calls. I certainly don't plan the type of future where we live like that. But I also don't want to presume that Theo wants to be in my bed tomorrow morning.

"Two," I reluctantly say. "For now."

"For now," she agrees, then goes to find fresh linens for the bedroom closest to mine.

***

I'm vibrating out of my skin on the carriage ride over. The sun has nearly set, and as we get closer and dusk has firmly set in, I leave the carriage and go the rest of the way on foot. No sense alerting anyone to my presence if Theo isn't ready to go.

He's going to be mine tonight. He's going to be mine forever, and the only thing between us and that happening is a piece of paper.

I'm head over heels obsessed with him already. He occupies every waking thought, and my nearly dead heart beats faster when he's around. I need him in my life, and I'm desperate to get to know what our forever will look like.

There's an ominous aura around the house as I draw closer. Nothing so obvious as something I can see, but I can feel it, nonetheless. Something is wrong.

It sets my nerves on edge and I begin to walk faster, determined to find my mate and get him out of there. I don't want him in there a second longer than necessary.

The scream breaks the air as I walk up the front path, and I run, heedless of Theo's desire for me to wait for him to walk out. Theo wanted to keep this quiet, but I won't stand for him being hurt.

That scream is his scream. I haven't heard it before, but I know it, deep in my soul. And I won't allow it. I won't let anyone hurt him ever again.

I break down the front door with my shoulder, barreling through it like tissue paper. There's another scream, and I follow the sound. The rational parts of me are gone, leaving me little better than a beast hunting prey.

Rowan stands over my mate with a bloody switch, and I see red. "What the fuck are you doing?" I seethe.

Theo's head spins, and I see the pain creasing his features and the fear in his eyes. He stares at me like he can't even contemplate my presence.

Rowan chuckles. "Wasting perfectly good blood, as far as you're concerned, although you're welcome to lick it off the floor." I freeze, sure Rowan has no idea just how badly he insulted me, and equally sure that I have no desire to give him the benefit of the doubt. Me, a prince of the realm, licking blood off the dirty floor. If he said that to my father, he'd have his head. "What the fuck are you doing in my house?"

"Stopping you. How dare you beat him?" I take a step closer, and if Rowan had any sense, he'd be afraid.

He seems devoid of sense entirely though, standing his ground and not even flinching when I flash my fangs. "A man has the right to treat his possessions however he feels is appropriate."

"Theo is a person."

"Theo is a human," he snarls. "He is practically dirt. Useful, but not worth very much."

I'd like to rip him apart for that, but my attention shifts when Theo screams out again. Only nothing is touching him this time, and his back bows and face twists like he's burning from the inside out.

When at last he stops, his chest is heaving, his skin a sweat-slicked mess, and when he meets my eyes something is different.

His eyes are clearer, and something about them seems stronger. It's his very presence, like he's more here than he ever was before. I take a stab that I know what that look really means.

"Theo," I ask, faking casualness as best I can, "do you want to leave this place?"

"Leave?" Rowan laughs. "He can't leave. Watch—Theo, scrub this blood off the floor."

Theo doesn't run to get cleaning supplies, though. Instead, he stands. It looks alarmingly painful, but he straightens to his full height and steps to my side.

"How?" Rowan sputters. His stoop-backed posture is suddenly more obvious as the man who looked so big wielding the switch is made small.

I almost rub it in his face, wanting him to know how Theo outsmarted him, but Theo jolts and I can read his train of thought easily enough. That girl who helped him is still in this house, and Theo doesn't want to leave her a mess to handle.

"You think money can't buy me spells of my own?" I say cooly. "Money opens a lot of doors. And when I want something, I get it." I turn to look at Theo, although I leave half my attention on Rowan. "We're leaving."

It's a herculean battle not to touch him, not to tenderly check his wounds and fret and worry. But I think I just gave Rowan the impression that I purchased Theo's spell, and perhaps it's safer for everyone right now if he continues to believe that I just want Theo for his blood.

Theo juts his chin out and nods, holding his head high with defiance as he walks ahead of me out the door.

"It's been a pleasure doing business with you," I tell Rowan, and then turn to follow Theo.

Chapter Nine

Theo

The carriage is not close by, an infuriating fact to learn when my back feels like it's been raked over hot coals.

"This is your version of a distraction?" Silas demands as we reach the end of the walk.

"Rowan only pays attention to me long enough to give me orders or to beat me. Ergo, it was the best option."

He huffs. "I don't know anything about tending a mortal's wounds, you know."

"I know enough."

"Do you need anything in that house?"

Marielle, I want to say, but don't. Silas' quick thinking saved her from being left in a terrible position, but I wish I wasn't leaving her at Rowan's mercy. I don't think he'll hurt her, not if he doesn't find out what she did, but he can make her life miserable in so many other ways.

I can't bring her. Not when I don't know where I'm going. "I don't own anything there."

"Well, you can't say that about where you're going," Silas says, voice filled with a false cheer that sounds decidedly out of character for him.

"And what do I own now, Silas?"

"Besides my heart?" he asks. "Anything you want. What do you want?"

"I want to sleep," I say. It's the only thing I can think of.

"Not until we get to the carriage. Preferably after we've looked over those wounds."

"You just said you don't know what you're doing."

"You can talk me through it, then. Tell me what I need to do."

"How far away is this damn carriage?" I huff. The raw skin on my back is pulling, and I wince with every step.

"Not that much further."

True to his word, it's parked beneath a big old tree after the bend in the road.

Silas has a footman who doesn't seem to be a vampire. His eyes glow, and his skin seems wispy at the edges, like he's going to fade away into shadows. He doesn't seem to talk much, just opening the door and closing it again once we're inside.

I shrug my ruined shirt off and turn so my back faces Silas. "Alright, have at it."

"Have at what? I told you, you need to tell me what to do."

I shake my head. "No, you said you like my blood. I'm bleeding. Might as well not waste it."

I chance a peek over my shoulder to see his reaction, and his lips are pursed into a frown. "I don't want your pain."

"So we'll let me be in pain but have it be worth nothing? You can't change it either way. And I chose this. I knew what pissing him off would do. I wanted this, if it meant I gave Marielle the distraction she needed."

He looks at me for another long moment, then sighs. "It might help, anyway," he mutters, like he needs to justify it to me. "I don't have anything humans use for healing, but my mouth is at least clean. I can't catch any of the normal human illnesses or diseases and pass those on to you. The only illnesses I can get are blood-born, and trust me, you'd know if I had one."

I don't think I would know, but I trust him regardless. "How do you want me?"

"Dangerous question," he purrs, the flirt in him returning. "For now, just as you are will work." And without any more hesitation, he leans forward and licks at the bloody wounds.

I groan, because anything touching the wounds doesn't feel great. But after a prolonged moment, it starts to feel... good. Like some sort of balm, maybe, a cool, soothing relief against the skin.

"You taste divine," Silas murmurs, his breath tickling my skin. "Like nothing, absolutely nothing, I've ever had before."

My eyes droop closed. Something about this is soothing, like he's lulling me to sleep. The pain slips away, the fear I've been carrying for so long dissipates, and my entire body collapses.

Silas' strong arms catch me. His mouth moves away from my back, causing me to whimper. "What is it, darling?"

"Nothing. Just tired. I—keep doing that," I mumble, my words slurred.

His hands stroke over my bare chest. "You rest, Theo. We'll be home when you wake."

Home. That sounds so nice. It doesn't even matter that it's not home yet. It could be home. I've never had that before.

My eyes slide closed. Silas keeps touching me, and for the first time in what feels like my entire life, I fall asleep.

CHAPTER TEN

SILAS

Theo did tell me that all he wants from freedom is to sleep, and now I can see just how exhausted he really is. It's like ending Rowan's hold on him has let his body finally relax, although I selfishly want to believe that my presence has something to do with it.

He shivered like I was sucking his cock when I licked the blood off his back. I wonder if he would actually respond well to me biting him.

When the carriage pulls up to the main gate, Jonathan opens the door. I nod once at the shade, carefully drawing Theo to my chest so I can carry him inside.

Deidre meets me at the door, wringing her hands. She's looking so much better, although these strange nerves are disconcerting. "Silas—"

"Shh," I whisper, looking pointedly at the sleeping human in my arms. "Later."

"Not later," she hisses, taking a step closer. "We have a guest."

"Who?" I demand, tightening my grip on Theo. Who the fuck would be here right now?

"Me," a voice booms from the doorway. It's a voice I only hear on rare occasions but nevertheless recognize immediately.

"Father," I murmur, knowing he can hear me. I hope he can't hear the nervousness in my voice. "What are you doing here?" Why is he here now? Why this night of all nights?

"Because three of my wives are dead, two of your brothers, and I barely escaped with my life," he snaps, stepping into the courtyard. He's never a quiet man, and I'm amazed that Theo doesn't wake up. "And I came here because you're the last remaining son I trust."

Deidre gives me a long look, her lips pursed, and I know she's heard it all already and that it isn't good. Five family members dead, and someone tried to kill our father? And he came here?

Deidre is stronger than she was, but she's not a fighter even when she's at her best. This is not a household of people who can stand against an army for him. And I'm holding a delicate, fragile human in need of some peace and safety in my arms.

That fact does not escape my father. "Who the fuck is that?"

I debate lying for a moment, but it's fruitless. He'll be able to sense the lie, and they'll all know that Theo is my mate soon enough. I won't hide him, even if I'd like a chance to prepare his protection a little better.

"Theo," I say shortly. "My mate. Who's in need of a place to sleep and recover. Excuse us."

No one leaves the king waiting, but I do, stepping around him entirely in order to bring Theo up to bed.

***

When Theo is comfortably tucked into his new bed, resting on his stomach so he won't put pressure on the wounds on his back, I spend a long moment watching him. He's at peace, completely out to the world.

He needs his rest desperately, so I look for another long moment and retreat before my father comes bursting in to disturb us both.

Deidre has at least kept him downstairs, the two of them in the more formal sitting room. I try to keep my head up as I walk in. This is my home. And yes, I only have it by the grace of my father. None of us truly own anything when everything really belongs to the king. But this is my home, my sister, my mate. He might be my king, but I have some ground to stand on here.

"What happened, father?" I ask, taking a seat opposite him.

Deidre sits in the armchair closest to the fire. Cold doesn't bother us, but Deidre has always been like some sort of cat, soaking up every inch of warmth she can get. Some days, I think she'd crawl into the sun if it wouldn't kill her.

"Jonas attempted a coup last night," he says. It's so matter-of-fact, like he's reporting on the weather. My whole body goes tense like a bowstring.

"A coup?" I ask, voice faint. Jonas has long been the favorite son, the firstborn and the one always at my father's side. What could he possibly hope to achieve? Could he really have been so desperate for a throne that he'd overthrow our father and force the entire kingdom into upheaval?

"He's dead," my father says coldly, like it's not his closest son he lost. "But he took out most everyone else present. Lark tried to stop him, and died in the attempt."

Lark's dead too. Lark is closer to my age, but a prodigious warrior and he's always been someone my father kept an eye on. But even his strength couldn't save him. "How'd Jonas do it?" I ask, trying to picture what could kill Lark.

"Fifteen hired assassins." He sounds like he's commenting on the weather while I'm left reeling.

"You survived," I manage to say, more out of surprise than anything.

"And you young shits should know not to challenge me," he says, eyes temporarily brightening with fury. "I always win."

He does. We all know it, too. He's not a cruel ruler, but he is indisputably the ruler. We all work under him, from sons like Lark and Jonas with massive stakes in his empire, huge holdings, and roles in governance, to children like Deidre and I, who barely exist on the fringes. And I've liked it that way, lord of an obscure plot of land and mostly left to my books and research. I knew my father ruled us all, and he left me be, and it all worked out.

"You came here." That's the piece I can't wrap my mind around. Why here?

"I'm in need of a new heir," he says simply. "And no one will look here for at least a little while."

I reel back. "And you came here?" I am the last son who he should have thought of. I have too many older brothers for him to have ever considered me.

If I wanted the throne, I would have been kissing his ass along with most of my siblings, hanging on his every word closer to home. But I'm here for a reason, and it's because I never wanted something like that.

He sighs, leaning back. "Too many of your siblings could be involved in this. Hell, my wives could be too, vying for their own sons. But you... you aren't."

"How do you know?" It's a stupid thing to say, to let this dangerous man think even for a minute that I'd willingly betray him. But I ask anyway.

"Because you're so far down the line of succession you have nothing to gain. Because you cried over a kitten when you were a boy. Because your mother raised you better than that and would kill you herself if she thought you were doing something like that. Because you went out of your way to save your sister when everyone had given up on her," he says, waving a hand dismissively. "You won't betray me. And, given your mother, you might actually make a good king someday."

My mother is a princess in her own right, the daughter of a small duchy before my father took control of all vampiric territory. I've never met anyone more noble and refined than my mother. She's been married to my father for a long time, but I am her only son. She acts more of a private advisor to my father than a lover these days, and I've never known someone with more steel in their spine. If anyone could make me someone people would want to follow, it would be her. Thankfully, she's never tried; she lives her own life in my father's house, and has always been content to let me lead mine. It's a system that's worked out for both of us.

"Take your pick of reasons. With Jonas dead, I'm in need of a new heir."

"Are you really, though? Given up on your plan to live forever?" I snark, unable to help myself.

Deidre makes a noise that sounds suspiciously like a laugh, although she disguises it with a cough. It's a weak gesture, given that we don't cough, but we all ignore it, regardless.

"Don't be smart with me. There always needs to be a plan."

"Find someone else." Moving to my father's home to be at his side is at the absolute bottom of my list of priorities. I like my home here. I like my life. And I especially want the future I've spent the last few days dreaming of with my mate.

Like he can read my mind of where my thoughts are going, he continues, "Of course, you'll need to get rid of that human."

I go entirely still, like all the blood in my body turned to ice. "Sacrilege, to speak of a mate like that."

"A human mate is a weakness, Silas. A distraction."

"He is my mate. And he doesn't have to be human forever. That's the beauty of our species." Vampirism is both a blessing and a curse, and I can bestow it on others for either purpose. Hopefully, with my mate, it's a blessing.

"He's common. You are above such things. You are the descendent of royalty, Silas. You don't lower yourself to common street trash."

I see red. I'm not prone to anger, typically more involved in intellectual pursuits than anything that would truly rile my passions, but I am ready to commit patricide now. "Spoken like a man who couldn't protect his mate."

Deidre hides her gasp and the air in the room goes deadly still. "Watch your mouth, boy," he says, every syllable dripping with promised threat.

"No, I don't think I will. Not in my own house."

"A house you occupy because I let you be here," he corrects.

"And what will you do about it now?" I challenge, pretending to look around. "Who's going to protect you if not for me?"

"If you think I need protecting—"

"I think one of your sons just tried to murder you," I remind him. "Don't threaten my mate again, or I'll be the second one today. And Jonas was an idiot, but I won't miss."

I stand, not deigning to give him a moment more of my time. I have a mate to look after.

CHAPTER ELEVEN

THEO

I wake up slowly, my body relaxed, and I think I'm still dreaming for a moment. This isn't real. Nothing like this is ever real.

But the linens—and since when do I have linens on my bed—smell like something that tickles my brain into wakefulness. They smell clean, and pleasantly spicy, and not at all floral.

Fuck, I hadn't even noticed how floral everything in that damn manor smelled. The absence of it forces me to open my eyes.

It's dark in here, with heavy curtains drawn across the windows. I sit up, trying to peer around the room, but the darkness obscures everything. "You're awake." I jump at the noise, not having even seen Silas sitting by the door, and press my hand to my chest.

"What are you doing?" I demand. I hear a match being struck, and then there's a candle illuminating the room. I don't let myself look around yet, though, instead staring at Silas' now-visible face. "Were you trying to give me a heart attack?"

"Don't joke like that," Silas mutters. He sets the candle aside on a little table by his chair.

I realize he's physically blocking the door with his body. "Worried I'll run away?"

He looks at the door behind him and then at me. "This isn't to keep you in. You can go anywhere you want to go, darling. This is to keep everyone else out."

"Why?" Is this place dangerous? Did he really bring me somewhere where I need a vampire guard watching over me while I sleep so nothing bad happens?

I'm thankful that I didn't let Marielle come with us, then. I have this sinking feeling inside me, realizing I've possibly misplaced my trust. Silas seems to want to protect me, but if he brought me to such a dangerous place, then I can't trust him to have my best interests at heart.

"My father came to visit. And he's frustrated that I won't give him what he wants, and I don't want him taking his frustration out on you."

"Is that... common?" I ask.

He raises an eyebrow. "When you have forty-seven children, warm and kind parenting simply isn't effective anymore."

"Forty-seven?" My voice is strangled at just the thought. Forty-seven children? I can't even imagine it.

Silas smiles, sharp teeth flashing. "Most species like me have trouble propagating. Vampires do too, in the traditional sense—but that never stopped my father. He's had many years and many wives to make it happen. Seems to believe in the myth of the largess of kings."

Forty-seven siblings. I can't even imagine that.

"What does he want?"

"An heir. His last one proved unsatisfactory, given he tried to kill him yesterday."

"What?" My voice is a barely there croak. What did I get myself into?

Silas is next to me on the bed before I can even blink. He sits on top of the thick blanket, leaving a modest distance between us, but his hand curls over the bare skin of my shoulder, finding an uninjured bit of skin there. "None of that will affect you."

"Right," I say hollowly, forcing myself to take deep breaths to calm myself. "I'm just the human. I'll stay out of the way."

Silas actually growls, an earthy, nerve-wracking sound at odds with his always refined appearance. "It won't affect you because I will slaughter anyone who bothers you about it, Theo. You are my mate. And that comes with my protection."

"In exchange for what?" I dare to finally ask the question I kept silent about before. Before, I wanted out of Rowan's clutches too badly to ask. Now, I need to know. "Sex? Blood?"

"Either, both, neither. Whatever's on offer," Silas says. His hand rubs gently at my shoulder. "And I mean that genuinely. You offer, darling. Absolutely no one, including me, demands. But all of that is irrelevant, because it's not an exchange. This is your home now. I am your mate. You don't owe me a single thing for that."

That's an absolutely ludicrous statement, but Silas sounds so sincere. Maybe he believes it himself, but that doesn't mean it's true.

I don't argue. "How long was I asleep?"

"Over an entire day. Not surprising, given everything. And sleep was the first thing you said you wanted with your freedom. Did I deliver, darling?"

"I've never slept in such a comfortable bed."

"If you think this bed is comfortable, you should try mine."

"This isn't yours?" I haven't examined every corner of the room yet, but the comfortable bed and soft, heavy blankets, the pillows that feel like clouds, the bed hangings and curtains that look like velvet, the gilded mirror and luxurious looking rug—I assumed this was Silas' room. No one spares this type of luxury on a guest.

"It took everything I had not to put you right into my bed," he admits. "But no. This room is yours, and no one else's, for as long as you want it to be. You control who comes, who goes, and what's inside it. It's all yours, darling."

"You came in," I point out.

"Forgive me. Would you like me to leave?" He goes as if to stand, like he'd really leave.

I reach out and snatch at his wrist, trying to hold him to me, before I even truly process what I'm doing. He stops moving. "Don't go."

"I won't." He turns my grip so he's holding my hand, stroking over the back of it slowly. "I won't go anywhere you don't want me to." He strokes my hand for another moment, the gesture almost meditative, but then he turns his attention back to my face. "Are you hungry?"

"Aren't you?" I ask, although yes, I am in fact hungry. Still, I've gotten so used to the feeling of hunger that it hardly matters anymore, and I'm more curious about him than I am hungry.

"No. Someone fed me some of the most delicious blood."

"That can't have been enough," I argue. Unless he took more than just the already-leaking wounds after I was unconscious?

His face darkens. "Rowan made you bleed plenty. And you'd be surprised how little my kind actually needs. We just need enough to refresh the supply in our body. Any stories of vampires glutting themselves on blood are unrealistic, although I can't guarantee that no one in my family has ever staged such a scene."

I don't know any stories about vampires because I know nothing about this whole world, but I decide not to remind him of that fact. "In that case, I could use a meal. Do you keep regular food here?"

"Not all the staff are vampires," he says. "Remember Jonathan, the shade who drove our carriage?" He tilts his head. "Bad example; shades don't eat either. But the point is, yes, we do have food. And Deidre and I ensured there would be plenty for you. If it's not to your liking, well, we tried our best. And we'll do better next time if you tell us what you like."

The type of food I like is the kind that fills my belly, and it's a rare delicacy in my world. "I'll eat anything. Show me where to go to prepare it."

"Not necessary. Margueritte cooks here, and she'll be more than happy to make you whatever you'd like. Come with me."

"I'm half naked," I point out, looking at my bare torso. And I know my trousers are patched beyond what is probably appropriate in this house, considering how put-together Silas always looks.

Silas' eyes seem to latch onto my bare chest, and he doesn't say anything for a long moment. "I'll find you something," he murmurs, and then he disappears from the room.

I climb out of the bed, and realize for the first time how unsteady my legs are. My whole body feels weak as a newborn animal. Is this the beating I took? The blood loss? The spell ending? Some combination of all three? All I know is I've never felt like this before.

And at the same time, I've never felt safe to feel like this before. I trust Silas. Perhaps it's unwise. It's certainly too fast, but I can't help it. I trust him.

Silas returns a moment later, carrying a pile of clothes in his arms. "We're not the same size," he says, already walking toward me, "but this will have to do for now. I'll have a tailor out here as soon as possible."

I realize then that he's bringing me his own clothes. Silas, who dresses like royalty even when no one's watching, even to kneel in the dirt with me, is willing to give me clothes from his own wardrobe.

This man is ridiculous, and the gesture is touching, even when I quickly realize how right he is about the clothes not being correctly sized for me. Silas is taller than me by a fair amount. At least his thin, sharp angles match my current bony, half-starved frame.

"Let me see your back before you dress," he insists, laying the pile of clothes on the bed and waiting for me to turn. He steps closer, and I feel his hand raise, but he doesn't touch the wounds. "I can find you a human doctor."

"I've never seen one before. I don't see why this time would be any different."

"What happened when he beat you before? There was a before, wasn't there?" he asks, voice heavy.

I swallow. Silas is showing more concern just standing there than I know what to do with. "Of course there was a before. Maybe not as many as you'd imagine, since I'd have to work hard to disobey him. But sometimes he gave orders that just weren't possible, and I was always to blame for that, not him. And most of the time, I went about my day after. If it got really bad, sometimes Marielle could help. She knows more about the healing properties of plants than I could ever hope to learn."

"I can find you an herbalist, then, if that would make you comfortable," he murmurs.

"Is it still bleeding?"

"No."

"Pus? Turning green or black?" I press.

"No," he says quickly, disgust clear in his voice.

"Then I'm fine."

He sighs but doesn't continue to argue with me. "I cleaned them when you slept. We'll clean them again later, but if you're so insistent that you're fine, let's get you fed."

My stomach growls, and Silas reaches over to hand me the clothes, actually managing a smile that doesn't look menacing as he does so. "Today, I shall be your valet."

"I think I'm more prepared to be yours."

"No. Never. That's not why you're here."

I suppress the desire to roll my eyes. I've heard him say it what feels like a hundred times now, and it still doesn't feel real. But I somehow believe him, regardless. There's something about Silas. He doesn't seem like much of a liar.

"Do you have one of those? A valet, I mean?" Is this man so incredibly wealthy he has people who literally dress him?

"I have. I don't currently. I find the eccentric scholar image is best served alone."

"Eccentric scholar?" I ask. Silas holds up a shirt so fine I think I might ruin it just by touching it. It's in a rich shade of burgundy, and my first hesitant touch confirms it's exactly as soft as it looks.

"I like books, and if I let people believe that that's all that I am, then I get left alone here. It works, or it did until my father showed up yesterday looking for sanctuary and a new heir he thinks he can trust." His hands smooth over my shoulders, petting the shirt into place. Despite the fabric covering any sign of them, Silas still manages to avoid my wounds with unerring accuracy.

"And what else are you, Silas?" I ask.

"Yours," he says simply. "The rest, you'll find out on your own time. Let's get you fed."

He leads me out of the room into a hallway almost as richly appointed as the room I just left. It's dark in here, with wall sconces lit only periodically. No doubt it's more than enough for a vampire's eyes, but mine will need some adjusting.

"Down here," he murmurs, leading me down a grand staircase into an ornate foyer. "I can give you a proper tour later, although honestly once you've seen the dining room you'll have seen the majority of the important bits, minus the library. There's a ballroom, several parlors and sitting rooms, all of that, but none of it is so important you need to see it right this moment. And the gardens, but if you don't want to see those, no one would blame you."

"I don't mind the gardens," I say, glancing around at stark portraits lining the wall. It's not gardens that hurt me at Rowan's home. "And what about your bedroom?" I realize how it sounds the moment I say it.

"That is available to you whenever you wish," he says, grinning at me. "But now—food first, hm?"

He leads the way to a dining room with a table that could comfortably fit twelve, hilarious in a home where no one eats. A young woman sits at one end of the table. She looks like Silas with darker hair, the same bony, sharp facial structure and thin features and too-knowing eyes. Her hair curls slightly, giving her a wild look, and I don't have to see her teeth to know that she's a vampire.

"My sister, Deidre," Silas says, doing a double-take when he looks at her. "What on earth are you doing?"

She looks down at the haphazard plate in front of her. "I wasn't sure what you told him. I didn't want to make things awkward."

"I know what you eat," I tell her.

"Good. Then you can have this plate." She slides the plate a seat to her left, much closer to a strange vampire than I'd like to sit, but I don't argue, just taking up the fork and knife.

The first bite is divine. I can't ever remember tasting food this rich. There's something sublime about the sauce on the meat, and I close my eyes to savor, temporarily forgetting the danger all around me.

"Father is upstairs?" Silas asks.

"Refuses to come out," Deidre says. "I'll deal with him later."

"It's not your job to make him feel better. Maybe he could use being miserable."

"Maybe. Leave it to me."

I open my eyes to peer around the table, trying to get a read on the situation. Silas is clearly not thrilled that his father is here—enough so that he sat guard in my bedroom—but both siblings seem relatively relaxed right now. Clearly, his presence isn't so alarming that they feel the need to panic.

If Silas is calm, then I can be calm. I think that and it takes me a second to understand. Silas talks about a mating bond like a mystic connection that he reveres, and it sounds far beyond my comprehension. Why, then, do I feel more and more connected to him with every moment that passes?

"Good?" Deidre asks, and it takes me a long moment to realize she's talking to me. She and Silas go quiet when they wait for me to respond, and I nod hesitantly, hoping that I'm not about to lose the rest of my meal.

Deidre smiles. Her teeth flash as she does, but unlike most of the smiles I see from her brother, there's no menace there. "I'm glad. Now, keep eating—you slept so long, you must be starving."

"Thank you," I make myself stop and say before I shove another bite into my mouth, "for the meal."

"No *thank yous,*" Silas murmurs, his hand once again finding my shoulder. "It's yours. This whole place is yours."

Deidre nods encouragingly. "Ask for whatever you need. We might not know a lot about eating, but we'll learn."

She says eating like it's some rare field of study she can't imagine, and I smile. "I appreciate it."

"While you eat," she says, leaning forward on her elbows as she watches me, "Can I interest you in some embarrassing stories about my brother?"

Chapter Twelve

Silas

I groan. "Deidre, leave him alone, he doesn't need—"

"He absolutely does," she interrupts. "He needs every tool that I can possibly give him to keep your giant ego in check."

Theo smiles slightly, then ducks his head to hide it, and the argument leaves me entirely. If it'll make Theo smile, then I won't argue. I still heave a hopefully convincing put-upon sigh, though. "Alright, Deidre. Do your worst."

She pretends to consider. "Do I tell you about the time he sat in a chair reading so long his clothes started to literally mold around him, or do I tell you about the time he wasn't paying attention because he was reading and fell right down the stairs?"

She's greatly exaggerating the first instance, although I'm embarrassed to say that the second story is very true.

"You weren't exaggerating when you said you liked books," Theo murmurs to me.

"Likes books? Theo, sweet, I'm afraid to say you have a harder job than most to compete for your mate's attention. He's obsessed. He lives all the way out here so no one will bother him and interrupt his reading."

"Theo will not have a hard time getting my attention," I protest.

"You say that now, but we'll see the first time you find a good story," Deidre taunts.

"I'd like to see the library," Theo volunteers shyly.

"You see? Theo and I will merely read together. Problem solved." And I'm sure, with time, my mate will learn a thousand ways to fully capture my attention when he wants it.

"I can barely read," Theo corrects me, then looks down at his plate like that's something to be ashamed of.

"That's fine. You have plenty of time to practice. Or, if you don't want to, you don't have to. I wouldn't mind reading out loud to you if you just want to hear a story." Deidre opens her mouth to say something, and I glare at her until she stops. Just because I've always gotten impatient while reading to others in the past doesn't mean I would with Theo.

If Theo laid his head in my lap and told me to read, I'd read the entire library to him before moving a muscle.

Theo smiles slightly, his cheeks flushing with delicious blood rising to the surface. I stare at him, entranced, while he holds perfectly still for a moment before turning to look at my sister.

"So, he fell down the stairs?"

I groan and throw myself back dramatically in my chair, but I don't interrupt. I could never interrupt something that brings out that little smile.

***

When Deidre is done spilling every embarrassing story she can think of, and Theo has eaten the entire plate, Deidre stands and flounces over to Theo, giving him a kiss on the cheek that makes his eyes go wide. "I think I'll very much like having you around here," she announces. "Feel free to find me at any time—I have thousands of stories. Are you still hungry?" Theo shakes his head and I frown. That plate looked filling, but I have a feeling Theo ate very little under Rowan's so-called care. Should I feed him more often than Margueritte recommended? How much does he actually need? "Good, good," Deidre continues, ignoring my inner turmoil. "You should get that tour out of my brother. And then perhaps a bath."

Theo flushes again. "I'm so sorry," he murmurs. "I know I'm not that clean, and your sense of smell—"

She waves him off before he really gets going, which is good, because I would hate to have to fight my own sister for insulting my mate. "For your back," she clarifies, and Theo just flushes more.

She does him the courtesy of ignoring his embarrassment, simply stepping over to me to kiss my cheek before turning to leave. "I'll check on father and keep him out of your hair for the rest of the day," she promises.

I ring the bell for a servant to come clean the table. Theo jumps slightly when he hears it, and I realize with a hint of guilt that he's used to being the one summoned. "If it helps," I murmur, "everyone who works here works here by choice, because we pay well. I promise."

"I'll get over it," Theo says.

Maybe. But it won't happen overnight, and I need to be more cognizant of the things that will upset him.

The servant arrives, an elf named Cari who's worked here since before Deidre came to live with me. "He's finished his meal," I say, gesturing to Theo's empty plate. "And we need a bath drawn up in his room."

She nods and moves quickly, which is good because the tour truly won't take that long. Yes, there are plenty of rooms in this place, but we use very few of them, and even fewer are actually interesting.

Still, I offer him my arm. "Shall we?"

***

We finish the tour back at his room, where there's a still-steaming bath waiting. My staff has perfect timing, and I make a mental note to thank them for it. Something about Theo tells me I should do that more often.

I clear my throat when Theo just stares. "I'll be waiting outside the door," I tell him. "I don't quite want to leave you alone with my father about the place, even if Deidre is distracting him. But absolutely take your time."

"Is your father that dangerous?"

My father demanding that I kill him echoes in my head, and I shake my head to dislodge the thought. "He's a dangerous man," I allow. "And he would try anything to get his way. But he won't touch you, you have my word."

Theo fiddles with the shirt I gave him, staring down and seemingly working up to something. I wait for him to actually say it. "You don't have to go. Stay. Please."

I jolt in surprise. "You sure?"

"I'm sure. If you're sure? I don't want to assume—"

"Theo," I interrupt firmly, "We do this at your pace. I am ready for anything you're ready for. I'd love to stay."

I'd love to join him in that bath, stroke over every inch of his body, tease him with slippery fingers, make him desperate for more. And that's a thought I need to suppress. That is not going at Theo's pace.

So instead of lusting after him to the point where he sees it on my face, I once more position my chair in front of the door and sit down. The candle from earlier is still burning, and I make a mental note to send someone to buy many more. No one who lives here needs as much light as Theo, and if I'm essentially confining him to the dark, then I should make it as easy as possible for him.

That won't be forever, but neither of us have dared broach the topic of changing him, and right now I'm terrified to do it. Theo just escaped someone using magic to change who he is. Will I ruin the little, delicate thing we have if I suggest it?

While I'm worrying about that, Theo is stripping off his clothes and laying them delicately on the bed, which provides a spectacular view of his naked ass. Fuck, I want to bite him there. I want to squeeze and bite and make him mine entirely, and the view is only tempered by forcing my eyes to trail up and see the scars on his back.

What was it he said earlier? No bleeding, no pus. No turning strange colors. He must still be fine.

Fuck, do humans worry this much all the time? Their short lives must be exhausting.

Finally, Theo slides into the bath. The distortion of the water should hide at least some of him from my eyes, but the lewd, surprised groan he lets out sends my overactive imagination spinning. "What?" I ask, my voice hoarse, and I find myself leaning forward in my chair, desperate to be closer to him.

"It's hot," he says, eyes closed and head tilting back.

"Too hot?" Who in this damned place knows how hot a human likes their bath water? What if I've inadvertently scalded him?

He shakes his head. "Just not used to it. Feels good." And with that, he lets himself slide down a little further in the tub, submerging most of his skin.

I bite my lip so I don't start to list all the little things he clearly considers luxuries that he can expect now. His baths will always be hot, his food rich and plentiful, his bed decadent, his clothes soft and without holes. But I suppose that's the type of thing he's going to learn through experience.

Theo seems to melt in the tub for a long moment, eyes closed and head thrown back, before he sighs again and picks up the soap left for him. It's a fragrant, lavender-scented bar, and he runs it over his hand for a moment, seemingly just studying it before he sets to washing himself.

"Let me clean your back?" I offer after watching him clean most of the rest of himself. "Make sure it stays clean. Wouldn't want anything to happen to it."

Theo nods lethargically. He might be relaxed, but I have never been more on edge in my entire life. My completely naked mate is going to let me touch him.

I move around to the back of the tub and kneel, ignoring the water that's dripping out onto the floor and staining my pant legs. I take the soap and the cloth from him, lather it up, and then urge him to lean forward so I can get to his back.

I try to be gentle, but he hisses in pain a few times, regardless. "I know, I'm sorry," I whisper.

He shakes his head. "I've had worse." He perks his head up. "What are you going to do if I did get an infection?"

"Treat it?" I ask, now worried he's hiding an infection from me. Of course I'll treat it. I wrack my brains for anything and everything I ever read about human medicine, which isn't nearly enough. Who would be most qualified to treat him?

"I mean, you said diseased blood was dangerous for you."

"Yes."

He vaguely gestures at his back. "It would be infected blood. You shouldn't be around that, just in case. I don't know how long it can take infections to appear to the naked eye."

My almost-dead heart starts beating twice as fast, an uncomfortable experience for someone used to it beating so slow. He's worried about me.

"The blood needs to get in my system for it to be a danger," I murmur. "And I already ingested yours." He winces at that, so I move the cloth off his wounds and instead stroke up and down his arms. It's meant to be soothing, but it makes him shiver. "It tasted delicious, Theo. Your blood is fine. We're keeping your wounds clean. But if you're worried, I'll get a human doctor out here."

He shakes his head. "I don't want to hurt you."

"You won't. Now, let me take care of you. Can I wash your hair?"

"What?"

"Your hair," I repeat, setting the washcloth aside for now. "Last thing to wash, darling. Can I do it?"

He hesitates a moment, torn on something. I'm desperate to ask, but I don't want to push him. He needs to know that he can make his own decisions and that I'll respect them. Finally he nods, and I raise a pitcher of water to his hair.

I protect his eyes with one hand as I pour the water on his hair, then set the pitcher aside and pick up the soap. I rub it between my hands to get a good lather, then start stroking it through his hair, scratching at the roots.

I wonder when the last time Theo got any amount of personal care was. Maybe it was never, or at least not within his memory. He's boneless under my hands, and I worry for a brief moment he'll slide beneath the water and drown.

I scrub at his hair as long as I reasonably can, basking in the peace I feel from him. Then I rinse his hair again, paying extra attention that the soap doesn't run into his eyes.

Theo's eyes remain closed and his shoulders relaxed when I finish, so I don't stop scratching at his scalp, massaging his hair. I want to keep him relaxed for as long as possible, but more selfishly, I want to keep touching him for as long as possible. I want to never take my hands off of him, and if he's going to let me, then I'm going to keep touching him like this.

I dare to let my hands move lower, rubbing at his neck and then his shoulders. His muscles are as dense as a rock, and I carefully apply pressure, trying to loosen the knots there so he can relax. Tension kept him safe where he was before, but he doesn't need that anymore.

Finally, the water has started to grow tepid, so I carefully withdraw my hands with the intent of helping Theo out of the tub so he can re-dress. As soon as I move, though, he groans in discontent. "Don't go."

I daringly lean forward and kiss the crown of his head. Fuck, he smells so good. "I'm not going anywhere," I promise. "Just going to get you out."

"Don't let me go."

Like I ever could. It takes everything in me not to hold him every minute of every day, and if he doesn't want me to fight that, then I certainly won't bother. "I won't," I promise. "But I want to get you out of there before you wrinkle up."

"Too late for that." Nevertheless, he stands, and I watch speechlessly as rivulets of water slosh down his body.

Fuck, but my mate is beautiful. He'll be even more beautiful when he's fed properly, but I've literally never seen anything more captivating than he is right at this moment. My mate. My Theo.

And he's half-hard for me, clearly having appreciated my touch. My mouth waters. "Theo?"

"Hm?" He doesn't look directly at me as he says it, and I force myself to hold still. He's not ready yet. He's unsure.

"I need you to tell me what you're looking for," I tell him firmly. "We're going at your pace, darling. And I need you to be specific."

"I don't want you to stop touching me."

"More specific," I rasp, because touching can mean so many things. So many delicious things, almost all of which I want to try out, but that doesn't mean Theo wants those things.

He shrugs. "I don't know. Just... don't stop. It feels real, when you're touching me."

A hug, then. A hug and maybe some petting, but he's not looking for anything else. I scold my cock, telling it to calm down and relax. It's not getting any action tonight.

My cock refuses to relent, but thankfully I think my jacket hides the worst of it. Theo doesn't ever need to know where my mind keeps straying.

I offer him a towel, determined to put another layer between the two of us. I'll hold him until the world ends, but a man can only be asked to endure so much. Holding him completely naked would drive me mad.

When he's wrapped up neatly, I take him in my arms and drag him back toward the bed, which was perhaps a poor choice on my part, but it's the only place comfortable enough to sit together. "It's all real," I promise him, unable to resist pressing a kiss to his neck. "And you can prove it's real because surely there's no dream where my damned sister would tell you every embarrassing story about me five minutes after meeting."

He chuckles, deep and joyful, and then says, "I liked hearing it. You're right; it made you seem more real. You've felt like a hallucination since that night you showed up, but now you're a real person." His voice is deep and languid, and I take a little more of his weight as he leans against me.

"I'm real," I promise him. "This is all real, darling."

"You might need to keep reminding me."

"I will. Forever, if need be." I hold my breath for a moment, because we haven't talked about forever as a concept yet and I'm not sure if now is the right moment. Forever probably doesn't mean much to the human who thought he was going to die at any moment. I don't say anything, waiting to hear if he's ready to talk about it.

He doesn't say anything, just leans further on me. I resume stroking his hair, since he seemed to enjoy it so much before. It works, but it causes him to slide further into my lap, where I can no longer hide my growing problem.

Theo hisses, and I worry it's a sign of disgust, but then he rocks again experimentally and sighs.

"Fuck," I mutter, entirely impulsive and entirely uncontrolled. My mate is rocking his ass against my cock; I couldn't control my reactions even if I wanted to.

But that doesn't mean that I'll let myself run wild with it; there are still rules here, after all. I grip his hips through the towel to hold him steady for a moment. "I need you to tell me what you're looking for," I remind him. "With words, darling."

And then Theo tilts his head back, staring me full in the eye with a hungry, wide-eyed look. "Touch me, Silas. Please. I want—make me feel."

And who am I to tell him no?

Chapter Thirteen

Theo

I've never been drunk, but I think it feels a little like this.

It feels like being half out of my mind yet aware of every inch of my body. My skin burns in the best way when he touches me, and I want to rid us of this towel, rip off his clothes so there can be nothing between us, and we can just touch and touch and touch.

Silas' intense eyes seem to rake over my whole body, taking in every inch of me. It's like he can see into me, see through me, and it sends a shiver down my spine. "You're in charge, darling," he rasps. "Show me what you want. Take what you want."

I discard the towel, having to wiggle in his lap to get rid of it entirely. Silas just groans when I move, but he doesn't try to stop me. He also doesn't try to push for more, although I bet I've teased him plenty tonight.

I've never had sex that I know of. Rowan, thankfully, had no interest in me that way, so this is something I know next to nothing about. There's some knowledge that sits in the back of my mind, the same way so many things have since I woke up under Rowan's control, like how to dress and bathe myself, how to sweep and even do little tasks like walking or eating. Fucking is in there somewhere, so I'm probably not entirely inexperienced, even if I don't remember any of that.

I feel inexperienced, though. I know the theory; I know where hands and cocks and bodies go, but I don't have any practice and every move I make feels clumsy. I begin to rip at Silas' shirt, then consciously gentle my hands, leery of how expensive it no doubt is.

"Use your words, darling," Silas croons, hands coming up to catch mine. "And I'll do whatever you want."

"Off," I manage to say.

Silas obeys, shedding his clothes with a lot less care than I was trying to show. When he's at last naked, I take him in, all lean lines and sharp angles. I can't see his cock from where I'm sitting, but it presses against me rather insistently. "What next?"

"Hold me." I'm already pushing him back so the two of us are laying down on the bed, bodies pressed entirely together.

Silas' skin isn't warm. It's not especially cold, but he's certainly not warm like a human would be. I vaguely remember what he told me about his heart pumping slower and him appearing little more than dead to a human, but while he might not be warm, his skin is soft and giving, his arms firm and strong. I sink into his embrace, closing my eyes and taking a deep breath.

This is real. It feels fake, but only because I never expected anyone to come save me. I was fully convinced I'd die under Rowan's cruel ownership. He'd bury me in his garden, and poor Marielle would think about me from time to time, forgetting me as she aged. I never expected to have any sort of life.

I certainly never expected an actual prince of vampires to come and whisk me away and ply me with luxuries. It feels like a dream, but Silas' arms help assure me it's very real.

I can feel his cock against my hip, even as Silas is clearly trying to hold perfectly still. Suddenly, it's very important that he knows that I feel the same. It's critical that I show him I'm desperate for him, too. Maybe I don't understand the mate idea he keeps talking about, but that doesn't stop me from wanting him.

Silas' groan sounds like it's ripped up from his very soul, which only causes me to rock against him again. I reach down and wrap my hand around my cock, curious to touch, to see if the reality matches the hazy impression of sensations locked somewhere in the back of my mind from before. Sure enough, the tip's wet.

I stroke that moisture along my shaft, tracing around the head before growing bored with my own cock. I might not have had any opportunities to be this turned on, but it's not like I'm unfamiliar with pieces of my own body. I want to touch Silas.

Like he can read my mind, Silas stops me with a hand around my wrist, moving so quickly that I haven't even touched him yet. "You do not have to do anything you don't want to," he says gravely.

"I'm very aware of that." Silas hasn't asked me for anything at all. I'm free. Every action I take is my own choice.

"Do you want to touch me?"

"Desperately."

Silas considers for a moment, then nods and releases my wrist. He makes a show of turning completely on his back, spreading his legs slightly and putting his hands up by his head. "I won't touch until you tell me what to do, if you want me to touch you at all," he says, voice deep and raspy, sending shivers down my spine. "But you can touch me however you want. I welcome your explorations."

His cock feels like velvet, and I stroke it for a moment, watching the precome bead at the tip. He makes a huffing noise, and my eyes snap from his cock to his face, just to find him watching me right back.

His eyes make something inside me unfurl, and his cock feels good in my hands, but it's not enough. I use my free hand to reach for one of his hands, stroking over the smooth skin there, so different from my own, and place his hand back in my hair.

It's not as good as when we were pressed skin-to-skin from shoulder to ankle, but his hand in my hair is soothing, and I want to keep exploring his body. He scratches at my head and moans when I circle the tip, bucking his hips slightly and tightening his grip in my hair to the point of pulling. It doesn't feel like getting dragged around by the hair when Rowan was angry with me, though. It feels like sparks, like my body is on fire and about to erupt, and I want to chase more.

"Fuck, darling," Silas mutters a moment later, hand once again tightening in my hair. "You feel so fucking good."

"I'm barely touching you," I dismiss. I might not know why I remember what I do about sex, but I do know that it usually consists of more than this.

He tugs my hair again, but this time with the purpose of getting me to look at him. "This is enough," he says firmly once I look into his eyes. His gaze is hungry, like he's starving and just for me. I shiver under his gaze. "This is everything, Theo. You have no idea how long I've waited for you. And I would wait forever, because this—fuck—this makes it all worth it." His eyes flutter shut for a moment when I stroke him from root to tip, running my thumb over the head, loving seeing how he reacts to me.

I love that he keeps reminding me. For so long, when I heard my own name, I'd tense up, knowing Rowan was about to utter some order I'd be compelled to follow. Now, I hear him say my name and my insides go soft with the care in his voice.

So I love that he keeps reminding me, but I don't plan to stop.

"Can I try something?" I ask, desperate to explore more, to know him so entirely that it feels like I have as much of him as he has of me.

"I already told you, darling—I'm yours. Explore away."

So, with permission granted, I bend my head and lick tentatively over the tip.

"Fuck me," Silas groans, and I glance up through my eyelashes to see his head fall back. With a concerted effort, he lifts it again so he can watch me.

I do it again, and watch as Silas's tongue dabs at his lower lip, mouth hung open slightly, eyes still captivated by me. His hand is still in my hair, but it's entirely lax, and I find that I don't want that. "You can tug," I tell him, reaching up to touch his wrist. "I like it."

"Fuck me," he murmurs again, voice sounding completely wrecked. He tugs my hair just slightly, as if testing the theory, and I lean closer to his cock again, humming my appreciation. Silas hisses and bucks his hips toward my face, groaning so deep in his throat that it causes the entire bed to tremble.

"What you do to me..." he murmurs, hips rocking slightly and seeking more. His hand tightens and releases and then tightens again in my hair. I think he's barely resisting the urge to tug me where he wants me, but right now I'm in control, and I lean down and suck just the tip between my lips.

Silas seems to lose control at that, groaning my name and squeezing my hair as his hips buck up and he spills down my throat. I pull back, letting some of it hit my tongue before the rest lands on my face and chest.

Silas lies on the bed for a moment, his body so still I'd worry he died if he hadn't already warned me that he doesn't need to breathe like I do. I swallow the come in my mouth and ignore the mess on my skin, crawling up over him to try to see how he's feeling. Why won't he say something?

"My turn," he rasps as soon as I lean over him, and he rolls me to my back and hovers over me before I really know what's happening. His movements are nearly frantic, but he pauses when he's over me. "Only what you want, Theo," he says, voice oddly calm. "Remember that. Tell me to stop."

I shake my head. Absolutely not. I want to see where this goes. I want to feel him, feel him on every inch of me. I want to stay in this moment forever, because this moment is real. "Don't stop," I whisper, and that's the permission Silas needs to continue.

He runs a finger through the mess he left on me, moving from my chin down my throat to my chest. "Messy boy," he murmurs, but it sounds almost like praise. "Let me make a bigger mess."

Then he settles between my thighs, spreading them gently with both hands to make room for himself. "Still okay?"

"Still okay," I promise.

"Good." He smiles impishly up at me, flashing sharp teeth. "I don't like having my hair pulled quite as much as you, darling, but if the need arises for you to grab on to something—I suppose I can make an exception." Then, without another word, he sucks my entire cock into his mouth.

Fuck, his mouth feels like heaven. He's so warm and wet and I can't control myself, my hips bucking wildly in the search of more. I never want to leave. I never want this to end, but I also can't think, can't imagine living in this exquisite perfection for another moment. It's too good. I'm going to lose control.

I fist the sheets instead of his hair, and his hands come down onto my hips, holding me still so he can expertly toy with me, using his tongue to make me see stars.

"Silas, I—" I groan, needing him to know what he's doing to me, needing him to know I'm losing my mind.

He pops off my cock. "Stop?"

Frustration boils inside me even as I'm frantically shaking my head. "No, no. More. Fuck, please, I—"

"No need to beg, darling, it's already yours," he promises, and then he takes me back in his mouth again and I lose control entirely.

He doesn't let me go when I'm coming, holding me in his warm, wet mouth. I try to watch him, to see how perfect he looks between my legs, but my eyes roll back into my head and I can't hold on any longer, surrendering myself entirely to the sensations Silas is giving me.

When I come down, Silas is petting my thighs gently. He smiles when he sees me looking. "There you are. Good?"

"Fuck." He laughs at me, but that's the only word I can summon the energy to say.

"I should clean you off again," Silas murmurs. "And then we should sleep. You definitely could use more sleep."

Some part of me wants to argue that I haven't been awake that long, certainly not a full day, but I'm asleep before Silas even gets the cloth.

CHAPTER FOURTEEN

SILAS

I spend half the day awake, just watching Theo sleep next to me.

He's beautiful in the throes of passion. He's beautiful all the time, but I could never have imagined a more perfect sight than Theo with his back bowed, his hips arching, face desperate for relief as he came down my throat.

I thought I'd seen it all, done it all, and if I hadn't, then I'd certainly read it all. But Theo is a new standard, and it's a standard that no one else could ever hope to live up to. Not that anyone else will ever get a chance to try.

I doze next to him a little later after checking his back one more time. The wounds are still clean and seem to be healing, so I let myself relax and sleep.

I wake up hard as stone, but unfortunately I know I can't ignore the elephant in the room any longer; I have to deal with my father's presence in my house. Showing Theo exactly how else I can make him feel good will have to wait.

I press a few kisses to his neck and shoulders, then reach for the bedside table. But where I expect to find paper and a pen there's nothing, because we're not in my room. If he wants to spend the days together more often, I'll have to see if he's amenable to changing rooms.

After dressing and sneaking back to my room for paper and a change of clothes for him, I leave a note telling him where I've gone and inviting him to rest as long as he wants or to explore to his heart's content. I debate warning him away from the wing my father is in, but I'll hear him coming and steer him away easily enough.

With another kiss to his cheek, I walk out of the room.

Being away from him leaves me feeling bereft. I've never worried about being warm before—that's not something vampires concern ourselves with. And yet I felt warm in Theo's embrace. I felt at peace. And being without him is like ripping all that away again.

I square my shoulders. It's probably for the best; I cannot be the cold, rational, conniving man I need to be in front of my father if I'm still wrapped up in thoughts of Theo.

I stop in the kitchen before making my way to my father's wing. "Theo will probably be up soon," I tell Margueritte. "He needs a big breakfast."

She nods. "That boy needs fattening up."

I grin. "He does."

"Especially if you're going to take his energy by feeding off him. He'll need to be strong for that."

The smile slides right off my face. "Not your business," I say shortly, a bit of a threat in my voice.

I'm not usually short with my staff. They make my life easier and I don't overlook that. But they do work for me, and I refuse to have them speculating on things Theo and I do in private.

She bows her head and doesn't say anything else, properly chastised. Satisfied that Theo will have breakfast and no unneeded comments, I walk off to find my father.

I knock once on his door, but don't wait for him to answer before I enter. It's my house, I remind myself as I square my shoulders. It's my house, and he is a king on the run from his own children.

He's sitting in an overstuffed armchair like he's been waiting for me. There's not a second seat for me, and I refuse to slouch on the bed, so I'm forced to remain standing like a child being scolded. I try to stand confidently, but it's a losing battle.

"What do you want?" he grouches, eyebrow raised as he takes me in.

"To know when you're planning on getting out of my house."

"My house," he snaps. "And I'll leave when I have an heir to take with me."

"It won't be me. I've never complained about my place here. I never asked to be your heir." I have plenty of older siblings. I've never deluded myself into thinking I'd ever see real power, and I've been happier for it. I don't need it. I like my life here, especially with my mate here now.

"Being an heir isn't about asking," he scoffs. "If you ask then you're unworthy. I am asking you."

"And I'm declining."

"You'd damn your kingdom?" He leans forward in his seat, watching me like a hawk, like he thinks he's won this argument.

I scoff. "You have plenty of children. Pick someone else."

"I'm saying it's you."

"No. Even if I wanted to, you ask a price that I won't pay."

His lip curls. "How is your new pet?"

I bristle, but I keep myself in check. He wants a reaction, I know. He wants to poke and prod and see me break. He wants to make me feel weak. "My mate is settling in nicely."

"How charming. You smell like the animal. Common and covered in his filth."

Theo ended up more covered in my come than I did in his, although there's no doubt I smell at least a little of what we did together. I can't tell if he's making a guess to get a reaction or if he can truly tell, but it doesn't matter. I'm not ashamed, regardless. This is my mate, and I'll celebrate everything we do together.

If I could scold my father into staying out of our business like I did Margueritte, then I would. But that won't work, so I settle for ensuring he knows I'm blissfully happy, regardless of his insults.

"Is there anything else?" I ask, faking boredom. "I'm sure you'd understand why I'd like to get back to my mate. Or not. I know it's been a long time for you."

I can see the anger in his eyes. It's there and gone, a flash, but it's real. It's the first genuine reaction I've gotten out of him. Perhaps I should feel bad about what I said, but I can't. Insulting him with his lost mate is a low blow, but I won't have him thinking my mate is fair game.

"Careful, boy," he murmurs. "I can still take this all away from you."

This is his house because he owns all the lands belonging to vampires. And usually that serves to keep me in line. But right now, I can see who has the power here.

"You came here to beg for sanctuary," I remind him. "Your own son tried to kill you. Either learn how to ask for help, or find yourself helpless and alone. It's your choice."

And then I turn to leave. I make it all the way to opening the door before he croaks, "Wait."

It sounds like it hurts him, and I take perverse pleasure keeping my hand on the door an extra moment, making him wait, before I turn back to him. "Yes?"

"Do you really think one of your brothers would be better for us all than I am?"

I watch him for a moment before responding, studying him. He seems almost smaller. "That's irrelevant. What I think won't change what's happening."

"I built this kingdom. I take care of my people. I made us rich."

"None of that matters right now."

He swallows, and I see, for the first time, an old man when I look at him. "Let's talk."

"Not if you mention my mate again," I warn him.

He nods. "That's fair. Sit down so we can talk. Please."

It's the please that does it. I wait a long minute, then nod, and concede to sitting on the bed so we can actually have a conversation.

Chapter Fifteen

Theo

I wake up in a panic. I don't know what I'm missing at first, but I'm missing something, and my body is desperate to reclaim it.

As lucidity washes over me, I realize I'm missing Silas. Silas is gone, Silas was just a dream, Silas wasn't ever real and I imagined the whole thing—

But no. I'm still in the soft bed, in the nice room at Silas' home. That thought sinks in and I calm down, which allows me to realize that there's a paper on the pillow next to me.

I scramble for it, and it takes me a long moment to read it, but Silas was kind enough to print it clearly for me. He's talking to his father. He told me to explore and to eat or to sleep, whatever I wanted. He's coming back. He's not gone.

I force myself to take deep breaths. It takes a long moment to regulate my breathing.

When I was with Rowan, I never panicked like this. I suppose there was no room for it then. But now, despite being safe, I can't stop worrying.

Going back to bed is completely out of the question. I still feel tired, despite getting two of the best night's sleep in my entire life, but sleeping without Silas feels wrong, like I'm leaving myself vulnerable. My body has decided that the difference in my sleep isn't that I'm finally free of Rowan, but rather that it's exclusively due to Silas.

So I get out of bed to look for my clothes from yesterday, only to find them replaced with a fresh, clean set of clothes. My heart feels somehow even bigger, like Silas can't help filling it every time he does anything. No one needs new clothes every day, especially when the ones from yesterday were barely used and still clean. But Silas made sure I had new clothes. And not just any clothes—his own clothes.

Silas must have also cleaned me up before he fell asleep, because although I dip the cloth into the cold bath water to quickly wash, there's not much to clean. And that's saying something, because if I remember correctly, I was positively covered last night.

I make my way out of the room, feeling naked without Silas. I'm supposed to serve in a house like this. Even before Rowan bought me, I wouldn't have belonged here. I might not remember, but I know it instinctively. I don't belong walking around this place like I have any right to be here.

The tour yesterday was a blur, but I do remember how to get to the dining room, and from there I'm sure I can find a kitchen. But when I get there, Deidre is once more sitting at the table with food in front of her.

"I know you don't eat," I remind her, which is probably not the politest greeting.

She chuckles, a deep, throaty, pretty sound. Deidre sounds like the type of person whose joy might be contagious. "I'm aware," she says. "But it smelled good when Margueritte brought it out, so I thought I'd take some. My sense of smell is significantly better than yours; smelling pleasant things is always a luxury."

I look at what she's pulled close to her. Fresh-baked bread and fruit that surely Silas must have paid a fortune to get here. She's pushed meat products away from her.

"Take a plate," she tells me, gesturing to the seat next to hers. "It was made for you, anyway."

I stiffen. "Silas said lots of staff here eat."

She shrugs. "They do, but not like this. This is the family table, Theo." She looks at me when she says it. *Because you're family now.*

I'm family here. They're trying so hard to take care of me.

"So, I heard Silas went to deal with our father," she says after I sit and make a plate for myself.

"That's what he told me."

She sighs. "He could be hours, then. Never heard a man who likes to hear himself talk more."

It's not my place to ask. I might be invited to eat at their table, but it's not my place to ask about their father. Nevertheless, I open my mouth anyway. "Your father. What's he like?"

"Don't worry about Silas. He can handle him."

It didn't truly occur to me to be worried about Silas. Something about Silas seems unflappable to me. I know that every man has weaknesses, and it's foolish for me to pretend that Silas is unbreakable. But Silas has been my strength, and I can't see him as anything else.

Deidre seems to realize that answer isn't satisfactory. "Our father is not a bad man," she says. "And he's been a good king. But kings are used to getting their way, and right now he wants something Silas won't give him. I don't think I've ever met two people more stubborn."

"Silas says he wants him to be his heir," I mention.

She shrugs. "Silas is apparently an inoffensive enough son that he doesn't seem like an active threat. And our father likes Silas' mother, which in our world can grant you a fair amount of power. It's archaic and barbaric, but when you have that many wives scheming at court, someone is bound to win favor. Our father thinks she might have raised Silas to have the appropriate temperament to be king. Which might have been true if it weren't for what else he's asking."

"What is he asking?" Silas hasn't mentioned anything else.

She hesitates a second. "You have to understand that our father lost his mate before any of us were ever born," she muses. "A long time ago, a child from a mated pair would be the favored child, but he didn't have an heir that way, so he adapted. He has dozens of political marriages, all meant to serve their purpose. Silas thinks it's jealousy. I think it's an old man's stubbornness in his ways, but either way, he's made it clear that if Silas accepts his offer, you are not part of the picture."

I swallow. It shouldn't surprise me. If I were a king, I'd also reject myself. I'm nobody. I can't bring anything to a king.

"So, Silas would have to... let me go," I say. It's not a question, but I see Deidre freeze instead of answering, regardless. "Kill me?" I guess, because that's the only thing I can think of.

Kill me? There's a king here who wants me dead, and my death is the only thing in between Silas and a throne? I know Silas doesn't want it, but that's only mildly assuring. The king wants me dead.

"Silas won't give you up," Deidre says softly. "You don't have to worry about that. He will die for you and do anything to protect you. Nothing in the world could convince him to get rid of you. And if our father wasn't so stubborn, he wouldn't ask him to. And none of it matters anyway, because Silas won't go with him."

"Being king is tempting," I say, even if I don't truly believe Silas thinks that.

She shakes her head, and something in her eyes flashes. "Silas doesn't have to be here, you know. In a house so old and out of the way. He's not in exile or anything. He's not an embarrassment shunted to the side. If anything, he's a well-raised child of two royal families with an impeccable education. He's smart and talented and his mother is well-liked by the king. Silas could have already had the type of honor he's being offered. He could have been one of the sons at the king's right hand. But he never sought that type of glory. He likes his peace. He likes his land and his books and the people he cares about most and being left alone."

I think I like that life too. Not that I get any say, and not that I get any options. But I'd choose a quiet, peaceful life here over anything else, too.

I study Deidre for a moment. "What do you think should happen?" I ask, because I can tell that she has more to say. Deidre sees more than she lets on.

She chuckles. "Oh, I'm not one of the children who'd be offered a spot at the king's side. I'm the last-born, my mother barely notable to the king, and I have other uses. No one listens to my thoughts."

"I do," I say softly. I could tell her that she's still a princess and that I'm barely a free man, but that's not why I'll listen to her. "I want to hear it."

She sucks a sharp breath. "Silas should be left here," she says. "He likes it and he tends to these holdings well, and the amount of knowledge in his head is more useful than turning him into a reluctant heir. Father needs to pick someone else. Someone entirely disconnected from the son who betrayed him and who's been away from court and their schemings. Someone who can give him an outside perspective and see everyone for who they are."

Someone like Deidre. She doesn't say it. I'm not even sure if she knows she described herself. But I hear it nonetheless.

"You should tell your brother that."

"Oh, I'm sure he and our father will work it all out. When they're done threatening each other."

My appetite goes a little cold, and I don't think it's just because this is more food than I've had in ages. "But Silas will be okay?"

"Your mate is the most stubborn man I know, Theo. He'll walk away just fine." She notes that I'm just pushing my food around now. "Join me in the library while we wait?"

I nod and stand to follow her. It feels wrong not to clear the table, but then again, it felt strange to eat at this table, and Deidre moves without a second thought for the dishes.

Deidre shows me the way to the library, gesturing around the room I only saw briefly yesterday. Even in that brief moment, though, it had been obvious that Silas loves this space.

"Read anything you'd like," she says. "Gods know Silas has a little bit of everything in here."

I move to poke around the shelves, and Deidre follows right behind me, clearly nosy about what I might choose. "Oh, I thought we got them all!" she says sharply, disrupting my concentration and making me jump. Her hand flashes in front of me to snatch a dirty handkerchief off the edge of the shelf. "So sorry you had to see that," she mumbles. "When I was sick, I was coughing up blood everywhere, and I wasn't the most considerate about where my handkerchiefs ended up. I'm so sorry; I thought we cleaned them all."

I couldn't care less about the mess; I'm hardly some noble guest they need to impress. But my eyes are captivated by the dried blood on the hand-kerchief. "I thought that blood could poison you," I say, already reaching to take the rag from her.

She pulls it back. "Holding it won't hurt me. It can only hurt inside me," she explains. "And it could hurt you worse than me. The human the blood originally came from—he died, Theo. He was very ill. So, please, be careful."

I don't reach for it again, but my mind starts turning.

There's a king in this house who's arguing for my death, and apparently some of his children want to kill him. I'm vulnerable and weak here, but for the first time, I don't have to be defenseless. I can hold my own.

And when Deidre sets the handkerchief aside as she starts her book, I pocket it.

Chapter Sixteen

Silas

I leave my father's rooms feeling exhausted but accomplished. And, despite being nearly three centuries old, I feel like I've just grown up somehow.

This is the first time I've confronted my father, and I feel like it's the first time he's seen me as an equal, as a man worthy of having a real conversation with. I held my own, and I made him hear me.

And now, all I want is my mate.

I find him in the library, and if it wasn't for my sister's presence, I'd probably ravish him right here. My mate, looking delectable and comfortable in my clothes, relaxing in my favorite place, holding a very good book on his lap.

Unfortunately, Deidre is the stubborn sort, and I know she's not going to let me throw her out so we can defile the library. I'll have to save that plan for another time.

But for now, I can steal my mate away. I hope my leaving this morning hasn't interrupted the mood we set the night before, because I'd dearly like to pick up exactly where we left off. I want to consume him and his cries of pleasure. I want to stay in our room until we're starving and are forced out for sustenance.

"Good book?" I ask, managing to sound like a functioning member of society instead of a desperate, sex-crazed madman. I honestly consider it an accomplishment.

He smiles up at me, using his thumb to mark his page. "Good enough. Are you done for now?"

"For now," I say heavily, because being done with my father's nonsense won't be an immediate thing. But there was progress, and I'll take a small victory.

Regardless, I have no desire to talk about any of that right now. My mind is so very far from my father.

From my sister, too, until she purposefully clears her throat rather obnoxiously. "Go undress him with your eyes somewhere else, please."

Theo blushes, but I don't wait for another invitation. "Gladly," I murmur, extending my hand to help Theo up and bring him back upstairs.

He automatically turns toward his bedroom, but I tug his hand towards mine. Perhaps it's too soon, but I'd like this to be our room. Our room, in our home, on our land. I like the sound of all of that. I like that vision of the future.

"How do you have even more books?" Theo murmurs, looking around once I open my door. I watch as he takes in the floor-to-ceiling bookshelves on two of the walls, and I confess there's another stack on the carved nightstand.

Most of the room is dominated by my bed, but there's also a chaise for reading and my own bathtub. I've spared no expense on this room. I like comfort.

"These are some personal favorites. But I didn't bring you up here to read." I stop in the middle of the room and consider what I just said. "Unless that's what you want to do. I won't force you to do anything you don't want."

He shakes his head. "Unless you want to read to me. I like listening to your voice."

"Oh?" I make a mental note to save that for later, because I definitely plan to take full advantage. "What else do you like?"

He looks at me for a moment, his eyes heavy, then snorts and shakes his head. Before my ego can be hurt, though, he says, "Do you know how ridiculous this magic is? I know last night wasn't my first time the same way I know I could ride a horse if asked, or that I know how to swim. But I couldn't tell you how or any of the specifics. I don't even know what to ask you for."

My heart aches for him a bit. I step closer. "I could show you?" I offer. "And you can tell me if you like things or not. We'll build your own personal repertoire back up, darling. Just for us." I can't help that last little possessive note. If I have my way, Theo won't ever need to sleep with anyone else, but we're not talking about that right now, and I worry my possessiveness ruined the moment.

Theo smiles. "Just for us," he agrees, and reaches out for me.

His hands find my stomach, and even through my shirt I can feel his heat. "Can you give me a place to start, darling?" I need to have an idea of where I can steer this.

He takes his hands off my stomach, only to grab my hands and move them to his hips. "Touch me," he murmurs, returning his hands to me.

I lean in, unable to help it. He's spell-binding. I take a long sniff at his neck, then press a kiss here. "Yes, I plan to," I tell him. "But do you want my hands, my mouth, or my cock? What will make you come the hardest for me, darling?"

A shiver passes through him. "Why don't you find out?"

He can't issue a challenge like that and not expect a response. I yank at the trousers he put my hands on, ripping them down the seams and not giving a fuck as the fabric flutters to the floor. He huffs but doesn't protest.

"I want you naked," I tell him, "Because I'm going to touch every inch of you. Lick you and suck you and stroke you and fuck you—" I press a few more kisses to his neck, just to emphasize my point. "You're going to be so overwhelmed with pleasure, darling."

"Promise?"

"Everything I tell you is a promise." I get my hands on his shirt, ripping at that next. "I promise to make you feel good. I promise to hold you and touch you and want you forever, Theo. Can I put you on the bed?"

He nods, so I walk us both backward, paying more attention to his skin under my tongue than the steps. When at last he falls back, I stand over him, feeling irrationally pleased to have him in my bed.

"This is our bed now," I tell him, voice low as I picture us waking up here together. I'll read to him like he asked, and I'll keep going until he gets impatient and knocks the book right out of my hand to roll me over and have his way with me. "Would you like that?"

"You want me here all the time?"

"If I had my way, you'd never be more than an arm's length away from me. So yes. I want to spend every night with you."

He bounces slightly, miming testing the mattress. "It seems as comfortable as the bed in the other room. I suppose it'll do." He gives me a cheeky little smile, and I can't help it anymore; I pounce on him.

"You're still too dressed," he murmurs, which is both true and too many words. I want Theo to feel so good that he forgets how to speak entirely. I want Theo strung out and desperate and blissful.

I press kisses up his chest to his neck, kissing and licking and sucking as I move. I aim to move toward his ear, but then he moans, "Bite me."

I freeze. "Theo?"

"Bite me," he says again, even clearer this time. "I think you want to."

Want is a mild and inadequate word, but that's hardly relevant right now. "I don't need to bite you," I say, stroking a hand down his side like he needs reassurance. "I don't need your blood. You're not here so I can have your blood. You're so much more than that."

He reaches a hand up to my face, turning me so I'm looking right into his serious eyes. "You told me you didn't have to make it hurt."

"Yes." True. My teeth are sharp enough to make a quick, clean puncture he would hardly feel, just a brief sting that I know full well I can distract him from.

"And you liked my blood, right?"

Another understatement. My mouth is aching the way it does when I've denied myself blood too long. I'm suddenly starving for him.

"Is it because of my back?" he asks. "Because if it's not showing signs of infection by now, and you've taken such good care of it, I'm probably fine, but I would understand if you're hesitant."

I kiss him to shut him up. "I'm not worried about that," I murmur against his lips. "I want you to know that you're not here to feed me. You've already been in one horrible place where they used you and drained you until you had nothing left. I won't be like that."

His thumb strokes my cheek. "I trust you." He looks almost surprised as he says it, then laughs slightly. "I never thought I'd say that to anyone, but I do. I know I'm just human—"

"—No just—"

"—But I swear I've felt something about you since the moment we met. I didn't understand it. I still don't, because I shouldn't feel this, but I know you. You are mine, right?"

"With my entire being," I promise him.

He nods. "And you would never hurt me?"

"Never."

"Then I wasn't wrong. And I trust you. So, Silas—bite me. Please."

"Fuck." The word slips out of me, low and hungry, but I still have control, and I won't hurt him. "I will," I promise him, "but not right this second. Let me make you feel good, darling. Can I? Touch you? Fuck you?"

He nods, his hand on my face tightening, trying to pull me down. I go easily, seeking his lips as he seeks mine. The kiss is deep and hungry, Theo seemingly desperate to consume me.

He pulls back and licks his lips. "You never cut me," he realizes slowly, eyes heavy as he talks. "You'd think you would, but you haven't yet."

"I have better control than that," I scoff. I suppose he could cut himself on the very tip of my fang if he tried, but I'm not going to actually cut him without putting a little effort in. I need to be deliberate, as precise as I possibly can be, when I actually do bite him so we both get pleasure out of it.

While he's distracted staring at my mouth, I shift my weight so I can have my hands free and begin to touch him, teasing and light until he's arching up against my hands. "You know you've had sex but don't remember the details?" I ask him. He nods, so I nod back. "Then you need to rediscover what you enjoy. So that's your task, darling. Tell me when I'm making you feel good. I want to know your body. I want to know how to make you melt for me, know how to make you scream and make your eyes roll back into your head. Are you ready for that?"

He nods, a fire lighting in his eyes, and I want to stroke it higher and higher. I want him to burn for me.

There's oil in my nightstand, and I reluctantly take my hands off of my mate to reach for it. Theo watches me with rapt attention when I coat my fingers.

"I'm going to try putting my fingers inside you," I inform him. "It's not something everyone enjoys, and that's fine. If you don't, then we'll stop." It'd be easier to keep control of myself enough to bite him if I'm the one inside him, but I'd be just as happy to have him inside me, or even take penetration off the table entirely for the time being. Whatever makes him feel comfortable and safe.

He doesn't protest, just nodding and watching my fingers as I reach down to open his legs and kneel between them. This would be easier with him on his stomach, but I don't want to lose his eyes. Theo says so much with just his eyes.

"Relax for me," I murmur, and then gently push one finger inside of him.

He makes a little huffing sound at the intrusion, but doesn't fight it or tell me to stop. I stare into his eyes, waiting for any signal that he doesn't like it, but it doesn't come.

I open him slowly, taking my sweet time. I have an eternity, and if I spend a thousand years right here, between Theo's thighs, you'll hear no complaints from me. Every twitch, every hitched breath, the way his thighs eventually fall further open—it's all pieces of the most beautiful picture I've ever seen.

He moans so beautifully when I rub at his prostate. "I know," I croon. "That feels good, doesn't it? Do you want more?"

"More," he agrees. "Like your cock."

"For someone who wasn't sure what you liked fifteen minutes ago, you seem to have figured it out," I tease. Judging by his flat stare, he's unamused by my comments, but judging by the way he rolls his hips against my hand, he's not so unamused he'd stop things.

I still my fingers and use my other hand to hold his hip. "Here's what's going to happen," I say, hoping he understands how serious I am right now. I wait until his eyes find mine, then continue. "I'm going to put my cock in you. Assuming you like it, I'll fuck you, and then, just when I have you on the edge, just when your whole body is ready to explode—I'll bite you." His blood will be pumping, his heart singing. He won't feel the pain of a bite then, and he'll taste even sweeter to me. "Are you okay with that?"

His only answer is rapid nodding, so I line my cock up and slowly push inside, giving him what we both want. His eyes close and his head falls backward, and I wait a long minute. Finally, he squeezes around me.

"Fuck."

"Move, Silas," he demands. "Please."

I can't resist a plea like that. I move, experimenting for a moment with the pace until I seem to find one that pleases Theo, judging by the groans coming from him and the fact that his eyes seem permanently half-lidded. He looks like some ancient deity, carnal and lusty and so fucking perfect. And he's here in our bed, with me, giving me the honor of being the one to give him pleasure. It's a heady feeling.

He starts to rock under me a bit, and then he whines, "Silas, I'm going to—"

Now. I need to do it now, when he's so high on pleasure even a pinprick of pain will be impossible to feel. Grinding against him, I lean forward, nose his neck to one side to give myself a better angle, and bite.

Fuck, he tastes like some sort of divine nectar. Definitely too good for the likes of me, Theo's blood is the sweetest, most pure thing I've ever tasted. I want more of him, need more of him. I take greedy gulps from his neck, glutting myself on his blood.

Theo makes a startled, desperate sort of sound, and I tense for a moment, but it's not pain. It's a wrecked moan, and then I feel him squeezing around my cock, because my mate is so godsdamn perfect that he comes with my cock in his ass and my teeth in his throat.

His head begins to thrash, and I carefully remove my teeth. I've been greedy, had more than my fill, and I can't risk hurting him when he thrashes about. Even with as much as I've had, I can't help but lick the inside of my mouth, chasing any remaining hint of his taste.

Fuck, I already want more.

The only thing that could compete with his blood is Theo himself, who comes down from his orgasm and seems to immediately dissolve into a puddle. Miraculously, I didn't blow my load inside him at the first taste of him, so I carefully withdraw my still-hard cock, not wanting to overstimulate Theo, who looks like he's had quite enough.

I stroke him, touching his arms and his chest and stomach, keeping the touch firm enough to not tease, trying to avoid any erogenous zones, just helping ground him back to earth. "Fuck me," he mutters after a long moment, and I can't help but smile.

"How're you feeling, darling?"

"So good. I just—I didn't expect it to be that good."

I almost ask what he did expect it to be like, but decide I rather not know right now. There are more important things to be focusing on. "Yeah? Glad I could be of service."

He raises a hand to swat me but misses entirely, his limp hand falling back to his side. "You're full of yourself."

"No, you're full of me," I correct.

"Not anymore. Did you come?" he asks.

"Not yet. It's fine. I got so much more out of that." That's an understatement. I'll never get the taste of him off my tongue. The way pleasure makes him even sweeter, brings out the brightest notes in his blood—it's unmatched. I'm spoiled forever.

He studies my face for a moment, clearly coming down from his high enough that he can actually see me. "You mean that."

"Of course I do."

"When I'm like you, you're going to lose that, aren't you?"

My heart jolts. When I'm like you. Not if, or any sort of hesitation. Just an assumption that it'll happen. We haven't talked about it, but Theo is planning for a future that will last forever. He's planning to literally change his species so we can have that future.

I don't deserve this man. I'm going to keep him, anyway.

Chapter Seventeen

Theo

Silas' eyes go all wide, and then he seems to take my question seriously, thinking it over. "Not really," he eventually says. One hand continues to stroke over my stomach, making absent little swirls and playing with the come there while he talks. I don't even think he realizes he's doing it.

"No?" I ask, pressing him for more. I'm still lost in a haze, my body floating separately from my mind. I want to float here forever, and I admit that I don't think anything but this current conversation could drag me back. But I've been wondering, and I want to know.

I've never planned for the future before, at least not in my memory. It's a novel experience, and if I'm going to do it, then I'm going to do it right. My future is mine now, and I want to know what options are on the table.

"I can still drink a vampire's blood," Silas says absently, almost mechanically. "It's less nutritious, so think of it as... hm. Perhaps like a human eating dessert, if that makes sense. It's more for the pleasure of it than the nutrients. And we don't do it often because there aren't many cases where it would be pleasurable, but with you, with my mate—that would be delicious."

"So, you'll still want me like that?" I ask, checking.

Silas swoops down to press kisses to my neck, licking over the bite mark he just left and making sparks light on my skin. "Darling, I want you in all ways I can get you forever. Don't ever doubt that." He goes silent for a moment, just burying his face in my neck. When he speaks again, his voice is soft and hesitant, something I haven't heard from him yet. "Do you want that future, Theo? To be like me?"

"Isn't that what's going to happen?" I ask, but I'm suddenly self-conscious that I've made more of this than it is. He keeps calling me his mate, keeps talking about creating some sort of life with me, but if he doesn't want me to be a vampire, then how much of a life can we even have?

I won't be the delicate, breakable little human he hides away. And even if I was willing to do that, I won't live very long. I'll live far longer here than I would have in Rowan's clutches, but human lifespans are still very finite.

Thinking about it makes my head hurt. Perhaps that's just the blood loss, but now I can't stop thinking about the future, and it leaves me reeling.

"It will happen if you want it to," Silas tells me fervently. "Of course it will, darling—I want forever with you. I just don't want to make any assumptions. You've had enough choices taken from you."

He's sweet, and I can't quite say how much I appreciate what he's saying. "I want that," I tell him. "Soon?"

"Whenever you want," he promises.

I almost say now, but I hold back. I want a few days as a free man first, to really enjoy being human. Besides, we should probably wait until Silas' father is no longer stalking around this house.

"Does that mean I can drink your blood too?" I ask him, and watch in fascination as his cock twitches.

"Don't say things like that if you don't want to get fucked," Silas scolds half-heartedly, voice deepening. "I would love that."

"Have you ever done that before?"

He wrinkles his nose. "No. Never."

"But you want to with me?"

"With all my heart." His hips rock again at just the thought, and I need to take pity on this poor man. I've kept him waiting for satisfaction long enough.

Unfortunately, Silas seems to have different plans. "I should get you something to eat," he murmurs, rolling off the bed and reaching for a truly decadent robe draped over the chaise. "I took enough blood from you, and I need to ensure you replenish that quickly."

He ties on his robe, which looks ridiculous with the obvious tent in the front. I can't help but laugh. "And what are you going to do about that?" I ask, pointing.

Silas looks down at his own erection, frowning, then shrugs. "Move quickly, I suppose. Avoid running into anyone."

"You ridiculous man." I haul myself up to sitting, ignoring the brief bout of light-headedness. "I'm fine. I'll be fine in a few minutes. Take a moment to take care of yourself first."

"Darling, I absolutely gorged myself on your blood like some wicked glutton. I've more than taken care of myself."

"I want your come," I tell him bluntly, hoping he gets the message. "I need you to come, Silas."

He goes very still for a moment, then says, "Well, when you put it that way..." before he throws off the robe and climbs back onto the bed. "Do you think you can manage to get on your hands and knees for me, darling?"

It takes me a moment, and finding my balance feels slightly more difficult than it should—not that I'll be telling Silas that—but I manage to find the right position. Silas shoves a few pillows under my hips to help me, and I spread my thighs, showing him my no-doubt well-fucked hole.

"No, darling. Close your legs." I can't imagine why, but I do as he asks. I've followed his lead so far and it's only led to pleasure, so I close my legs and wait.

I hear him fiddling with the oil again, and then his slick cock slides between my thighs, nestling into their tight grip.

He makes a few short, aborted little thrusts, leaning down and pressing some of his weight along my back. "I don't want you to be too sore later, and anyway I'm not going to last very long," he pants. "Let me fuck these gorgeous thighs, hm?"

"Whatever you want," I promise, rocking slightly with his movements.

"Tighten your thighs—yes, like that," he groans, thrusting between my thighs. "Your skin is so damned soft." His lips find my neck again. He doesn't bite, just presses soft kisses to the skin there, like he's reminding me of what we just did, like I could ever forget. He sucks on my skin, eliciting a moan from me. "Do you think you could come again?"

The most rational parts of my mind says of course not, but those parts don't seem to exist when Silas and I are like this. I nod my head, and Silas finds my cock with one hand, trailing his hand down my stomach first to scoop up the last of the drying come, slicking his grip with it as he strokes me.

"Come with me," he murmurs, lips right at my ear now. "Come with me, Theo, do this with me, don't make me come alone—"

How can I possibly resist that? His fingers twist over the head of my cock, and I'm coming, and Silas rocks against me twice more before he's coming too.

"So good for me," he groans, "So perfect, darling, a fucking dream—"

I want to tell him that he's the dream, that he is literally more than I ever could have dreamed for myself, but I'm too out of breath to get the words out. I collapse forward, the pillows beneath my hips taking my full weight, and Silas melts along my spine.

We lay there like that for a long moment, soaking in the bliss of the moment. Earlier, Silas asked if I'd consider moving into this room. I can now unequivocally say this bed is my favorite place on earth.

Silas groans and pushes himself up, reaching for his robe once more. "Now it's time to feed you," he says, and is out the door before I can protest.

***

Silas takes feeding me very seriously. I don't know if this is because I fed him with my blood, or if he's always this solicitous, but he feeds me bites of pastry and cheese and more of the fruit from breakfast. "I'm not actually that hungry, you know," I tell him, turning my head away from yet another bite.

He frowns. "You need energy. Replenishing that blood will take a lot out of your body."

"How often do you need blood?" I ask.

He pokes my nose instead of feeding me the piece of fruit. "Less often than you need to eat, and more often than you could safely handle feeding me. So get that thought out of your head."

The fact that he knew I was hoping I could feed him is astounding. "It feels good, you know," I argue half-heartedly.

"Oh, I know I can make it feel good," he says, and I have a brief flash of jealousy for anyone else he's made feel this way. "But I wouldn't trust you to walk in a straight line down the hallway right now, so you'll have to wait to feel that again, darling. And I'll get my blood in more mundane ways in the meantime."

"You don't..." I don't know how to phrase what I'm asking, but Silas just waits with a raised eyebrow. "You don't do that every time, right?"

He's quiet for a second. "I won't lie and pretend I've never done that in the past, although I can assure you that it's something else entirely when I'm with you. But no, Theo. I don't need to have sex with someone to take their blood. And I won't ever again. That's just for us now."

I suppose I can live with that. Silas holds out yet more fruit, and to appease him, I take another bite.

His other hand comes up to cup my face, tilting me so I'm looking at him. He studies my face for a long moment, then murmurs, "If you're tired, you should sleep."

"It's barely mid-day."

"Midnight, technically," he corrects. "You've adjusted to the nocturnal schedule far easier than I actually would have expected. And who cares what time it is? You can sleep whenever you need to sleep, darling. Absolutely nothing will happen if you choose to sleep the night away."

Right. I keep forgetting that I've technically switched to a completely nocturnal schedule, and likely will have one for the rest of my life. Most of the windows here are covered, and I haven't been outside since I arrived.

I should probably do that soon, before I feel like some sort of spoiled, lazy shut-in. But not right now. Now, I'm going to take Silas' advice and sleep.

"Will you lay down with me?" I ask.

Silas sets the food aside and sheds his robe, lying down with me completely naked and pulling me into the curve of his body. "Of course, darling. Let me watch over you while you sleep."

CHAPTER EIGHTEEN

SILAS

Theo sleeps the rest of the night and the entire day away. I wonder at what point I should worry, because while I meant it when I said he could sleep the nights away and no one would judge him, surely this is an excessive amount of sleep over the past few days. I really should consult a human doctor for him.

I also need to find a tailor, and unfortunately, while I have many people on staff here at the house, a tailor isn't one of the positions we've hired on. That seems like an oversight now, but I can at least kill two birds with one stone and consult a doctor about Theo's sleep and his wounds while I find a tailor who will come out here to get his measurements and make him a wardrobe of his own.

I enjoy seeing him in my clothes, but Theo deserves clothes all his own. Nice clothes, made exactly to fit him and exactly how he likes them and as grand as anything some wealthy lord might wear.

I should see a jeweler too. No one will ever question Theo's wealth and status again.

So, with another note and a lingering kiss on his forehead, I leave.

Deidre is still in the library, curled up with a thick political treatise. "Yes?" she asks when I step through the door.

"I'm going out. Keep an eye on things here, yeah?"

She nods, eyes still on her book. "I suppose. Is Theo awake? He's good company."

"Asleep, I'm afraid. You'll have to make do with Father."

She deigns to look up from her book at that, making a face. "I'd rather read alone."

I snort. I wonder how she's going to feel when I tell her of the conversation I had with our father yesterday. I wonder if she'll hate me.

But that's a problem for later. "Anything interesting in that book?"

She flips a page disinterestedly. "Men always seem to think everything they say is a revelation, and never will say it in one word when they can write a chapter instead. Tedious."

She's not wrong. "So, that's a no?"

"It's a no. You need better books."

"Perhaps I'll look when I'm out today." Not likely, since not even books can make me want to stay away from Theo a moment longer than I have to. "I'll be back before dawn. When he wakes up, please make sure he eats. He keeps telling me he's not hungry, but he should eat more."

"I'll tell your grown mate you think he should eat more," she says, smirking up at me.

"Thank you." I ignore her sarcasm and retreat, knowing that Theo is in good hands while I'm out.

The sun has barely set, which is perfect. The sooner I leave, the sooner I can return, and the sooner I return, the sooner I can hold Theo once more.

***

The doctor requires careful handling, because the man is entirely human and I don't want to have to kill him for knowing too much. But I explain my friend has been whipped, and explain the condition of the wounds, the blood loss, and the exhaustion. He finds it strange that I'm visiting without the patient, but I offer him more money than he makes in a month, so he doesn't ask additional questions and concedes that Theo is very likely just healing, but I should continue to watch the wound for signs of infection.

The tailor grumbles about the idea of travel, but when I plunk a purse filled to bursting on his counter, he agrees to come by in two days without any more complaints.

Business done, and with hours to go before dawn, I direct Jonathan back to the house.

***

Theo is in the dining room, eating another meal. Good. He looks up at me, a half-smile on his face that makes my heart beat faster. "Deidre informed me I was directed to eat, and that I was welcome to read with her if I stayed quiet," he tells me. That does sound like my sister. "You'll be happy to know that this is my third meal in one day." He says it like it's ludicrous, but even I know that, for creatures that eat, three meals in a day is very normal.

"Good job, darling." I walk over to him for a kiss, which he eagerly accepts. "What have you done with your time?"

He shifts in his chair and looks away. Odd. I frown, trying to catch his eye, but he doesn't look back. "Theo?"

"It's nothing," he murmurs, still not looking at me. It hurts me to do it, but I drop it. I remind myself he's been under Rowan's control for years now, where he would be physically beaten when he broke a supposed rule. There's likely some lingering scars, and not just the ones on his back. And if

I have work left to do in showing Theo that he's allowed to do anything he wants around here, well, that's my work. And I'm happy to do it.

I sit down at the table with him. "Well, what would you like to do with the rest of the evening?"

"Can we go outside?"

"I thought humans didn't like to be outside at night." They all seem to flee for their homes the moment the sun sets, only those forced out by circumstance—and therefore the easiest prey for creatures like me—left out.

He nudges me. "Well, I have my own personal vampire protector from whatever monsters might lurk in the dark."

"Let's go outside then," I say, feeling my chest irrationally puff up at his comment. "Do you have a particular task in mind?"

He shakes his head. "Just to see. It's not good for people to be cooped up inside for too long."

"Wouldn't want people to say I deprived you. Should I get a candle?"

"Is the moon out tonight?"

"Mhm."

"Then I'll be fine." He pushes his plate away and leads the way to the front door, but I steer him toward the side. "If you're alright being in a garden, then let me take you somewhere beautiful." I stop before moving any further, waiting for him to approve. I wouldn't blame him if he never wanted to see a plant again.

But he just nods, a small smile taking my breath away. "Show me."

So I take him to the well-manicured back garden, full of lush trees and overflowing shrubbery and rich flower beds. I think sometimes humans see my home up on the hill and wonder what sort of monster lives up there, but this garden at least gives me a small space where I believe it could be a fairy story instead.

"Beautiful," Theo breathes, turning in place to take it all in. I take his hand to guide him to a bench that will provide a great view of the grounds and the moon.

"It is," I agree, watching him instead of the sky. The sky is nice enough, I suppose, but it's not anything special. What is special is my mate. His wide-eyed, captivated innocence makes my heart ache for him.

"Marielle would love this garden," he says after a long moment, and the change in topic takes a second for me to catch up.

"Oh?" I ask neutrally. He says Marielle was kind to him, that she's not like her father. She's clearly important enough to him if he's still talking about her now.

"She grew most of the garden at the manor," he says. "The flowers, I mean." I remember them. They'd bloomed even at night, and they'd been beautiful.

"Do you want to see her again?" I ask.

He hesitates for a moment, then says, "I wanted to ask you to bring her here. She deserves to escape Rowan just as much as I did. But I didn't want to before I knew it was safe here."

It shouldn't hurt like it does. Of course he was worried if this place would be safe. Of course he had fears. It'd be more concerning if he didn't. Even so, it hurts to think that there was ever a situation when I didn't make my mate feel entirely safe and secure.

"And now?" I ask. "Is it safe now?"

"Not with your father here," he says. "Once he's gone, I'd like it if she came. If you're okay with it."

I almost say my father won't hurt her. My father won't hurt Theo either, despite his threats. But he'd respect Marielle more than Theo, even if he only truly respects vampires. I don't say it, though. Theo is entitled to feel threatened by my father's presence here. Hopefully, he'll be gone soon, so Theo can feel safe.

"Whatever you want," I tell him.

He smiles. "I suppose she can have my old room. Since I'm moving into yours."

Well, that does make me feel better. "Too close to ours," I disagree. "Wouldn't want her to hear anything inappropriate. We'll put her close to Deidre."

"Deidre would be good for her," he agrees. He looks up again, then squeezes my hand. "You're okay with it, right?"

"I am okay with anything and everything that would make you happy." I would become my father's heir if Theo wanted the prestige of that. I would conquer entire countries for him. Adding another younger sister to our household is a small price to pay for his happiness.

Margueritte comes running out of the house at high speed. "Sir, you have a visitor."

My head snaps up. "A visitor?" Who would come here? The only one I've invited is the tailor, and he won't show up for several days.

Margueritte nods. "One of your father's wives."

My muscles lock with tension. How did she even know to come here? What does she want?

"I'll be right there," I sigh, knowing the night with my mate is ruined now.

I stand and offer him my hand, but he hesitates. "Can I stay here for a moment?" he asks. "I won't wander off or anything. Just want to see the stars."

I don't love the idea of him being out here alone, but that's paranoia, and I won't lock my mate in the house because of it. "Alright," I murmur. "I'll be back as quickly as I can."

"Do what you have to." He turns his face up for a kiss, and my heart flutters at him clearly wanting me. I kiss him for perhaps a moment longer than I should, and then go to deal with my guest.

Someone has let her into the foyer, but Deidre waits with her, arms crossed and expression unimpressed, stopping her from going any further. "Donatella," she says. "Here to see Father."

I look her over critically. Donatella has been a part of our father's life longer than I've been alive, and she has four children with him. She looks travel-worn and impatient, with her eyes darting up the stairs continuously.

"What do you want?"

"To see my husband," she huffs. "Honestly, what else?"

"You came all the way here? Alone?" I press, not convinced. My father's many wives are all strong, noble women in their own right, but being taken care of by the king has left them mostly sedentary. I can't think of the last time one of them left court like this. And they certainly don't do it for something as trivial as missing him. They don't miss my father; they use him, and he uses them in turn, and everyone walks away with what they want.

"You have no right to keep me from him—"

"I have every right," I say coldly. "This is my house."

She sniffs. "By your father's kindness, perhaps."

I'm getting very tired of hearing that. I'm getting very tired of her presence, really, and am about to throw her out when a scream pierces the air.

"Deidre," I shout, already turning to run toward the scream. There's only one person that can be.

"I've got her." I barely hear what she says, already running for the garden.

Something is very wrong. Donatella shouldn't be here, and no one should be outside making Theo scream. I push myself faster, needing to get to my mate.

Theo's not on the bench. I put on more speed, skidding to a stop when I see him among the bushes with a dark form bending over him.

Isaac. The brother who perhaps should have been next in line if Father didn't come to me, and Donatella's eldest son. I freeze, and he stands, dragging a limp Theo up in front of him like a shield.

Blood glints on his face in repulsive rivulets. "What did you do?" I demand, voice barely a breath. All the air has been stolen from me, and my body begins to shut down everything unnecessary, only able to pay attention to Theo. "What the fuck did you do, Isaac?"

"He can still be saved," Isaac says, a perverse grin splitting his face. "But probably not for much longer. Bad luck to get a human—they bleed out so easily."

"What did he do to you?" I try to inch closer, but Isaac tightens his grip on Theo when I do, and I stop, unable to bear the idea of him hurting Theo.

Isaac shrugs. "Tell you the truth, I was going to leave him alone. But he screamed when he saw me, and I had to do something to shut him up. Couldn't have you getting in my way. And it works out now—you need to choose. I drop him and you might still be able to save him, but you can't have both him and me. Let me go take care of our father, and you can keep your mate."

My heart is in my throat, but it's no contest. Our father can fend for himself. Isaac can have anything he wants if he gives me Theo.

"Alright," I agree, taking a step back so he sees that I mean him no harm. I start walking to the side, clearing the path between him and the door. "Your mother is in there."

He watches me like a hawk. "She was meant to get you out of the way. Oh well. This works just as well."

My blood boils at his cavalier attitude. My mate is bleeding out. Some part of me processes that Theo is dying, his throat ripped open and who knows what else done to him. He'll die unless I can get to him and turn him into a vampire.

I take another step to the side, hopefully clearing the way fully for Isaac. And then Theo opens his eyes.

CHAPTER NINETEEN

THEO

I know I'm only going to get one chance at this, but I also know that he doesn't think a human is any threat to him. From the minute he attacked me, he hasn't spared a single thought for me.

I taught Marielle to fight this way too, to count on being underestimated and to use it. It's his mistake, and I hope he realizes that.

It takes more strength than I thought it would to withdraw the knife I stole earlier today, but I get it out of my boot, slumped over as I am, and, ignoring the burning pain through my whole body, stab him in the stomach.

He drops me onto the ground, and the shock of the fall knocks the breath completely out of me. I manage to grin up at him. "I killed you," I announce, my voice barely audible, but I know the two vampires hear it, anyway.

He raises his left hand to the wound, pressing briefly. "You mildly annoyed me. Your dying act," he croons mockingly.

I huff out a laugh that makes my whole body shake with pain. "I hear blood poisoning is a terrible way to go," I manage to say before I can't make any more words come.

Deidre's handkerchief, a glass of water, and a stolen knife. That was all it took to have a blade coated in a poison even vampires fear. I thought it was in case Silas' father tried to threaten me again, but this works too.

"What?" Isaac demands, but I can't answer him.

I laugh again, unable to help it even as much as it hurts. I look at this man who came here to murder a king, who probably considered me nothing more than a bargaining chip, who's going to die because of a human.

Good riddance.

I close my eyes, squeezing them shut. The pain is burning, consuming my entire body. I don't worry about that, though—I'll worry when I stop feeling it. As long as I can feel the pain, then I'm still alive.

"You heard him," Silas murmurs, voice closer than I expect. "You're dying now. My mate made sure of that. The only question is do I let nature take its course, or do I show you mercy and speed it up?"

"I—" Issac begins, taking a few steps back, but Silas is faster and more determined. I turn my head away, not wanting to watch, but the noises are enough.

And then Silas kneels at my side, gently moving my head onto his lap as his hands smooth over my skin like he needs to find my wounds. He doesn't need to find them; my wounds are painfully obvious to both of us.

"Do you still want this, darling?" Silas murmurs. His hands shake against me but he keeps moving them, like he's determined to touch all of me. "Is a life like mine still something you'd accept?"

"As long as you're in it," I croak, "I'll take anything."

"Good." He touches my face with the very tips of his fingers. "This will hurt. Are you up for that?"

What other choice do I have? Die? I'm not willing to take that option. Not when I just got a chance at a real life.

"Do it." I don't know what it entails. I don't know how bad the pain will be, although it can't be worse than dying right now feels. All I know is that I get Silas at the end of this, and I have to do whatever it takes to get that future.

Silas leans closer, his mouth latching onto the already-present wound on my neck, and I mercifully pass out.

CHAPTER TWENTY

SILAS

I have to drain nearly all his human blood for the vampire blood to be able to take. I can let him continue to bleed out slowly, or I can speed the process along.

I feel him go limp in my arms, and I have to fight every instinct so I don't stop. If I stop, then I risk losing him, and I promised him forever. I have to kill him to save him, and I don't know if I'll be able to forgive myself after.

I won't pretend that I've never drained every drop of blood from a living creature before, but I find it largely gross and haven't done it in decades. I have to force myself to keep going, Theo's human blood going sour as his lungs and heart stop providing the rich life force he used to have.

He'll never have it again, but he'll have so much more. I'll make sure he does. I'll give him a future he could never even dream of, make sure he has everything he's ever wanted. He'll have peace and safety and so, so much love.

His heart stops, and it feels like my heart stops with it when I feel my mate essentially die in my arms, but I can't give into despair. This is where the real work starts.

I bite my wrists open. I don't bother with finesse or making any sort of neat cut that will heal quickly. The more I bleed, the better his chances are. I hold one to his mouth, pushing the blood down his throat. I press my other gushing wrist to his wound, hoping some of the blood will get into his system. The more vampiric blood I can get in him, and the faster I can do it, the better off he'll be.

It's a delicate dance, but I'm a frantic mess. He has to die before the vampirism can take, and the more of my blood he gets, the easier it will be on him. But if I wait too long, he won't just be dead; he'll be gone, and nothing I could do would bring him back.

"C'mon, darling," I urge, even knowing he can't hear me like this. "C'mon, love. Take the blood, that's it. You can do this."

His heart beats again. It's one beat, slow and staggered, but I nearly cry with relief. He'll survive. The vampire blood is starting to work.

Now all he needs is enough blood to live. He can start with mine. I'll give him everything I have. But eventually, he'll need more than I can give him.

"Here," Deidre says. I startle, not having heard her come up behind me. She kneels down with wrists already dripping blood, pushing me aside so she can place her own wrists in Theo's mouth.

"Thank you," I rasp.

She looks over. "Isaac?"

"Dead."

"I can see that."

I forgot his body was right there. To tell the truth, I forgot everything except Theo. I swallow and manage to ask, "Father?"

"I took care of Donatella. Not until I got her to admit they came here with a plan to kill father. No surprise, Isaac was in on the original attempt, and this was his second try. She's dead." She shrugs, then tilts Theo's head so he can get more blood. I tense when she touches him, but force myself to let it go. "Father didn't even know until it was over. He came down, but I left to find you."

"He'll need more," I mumble. "And then he'll need blood with actual nutrition." Fuck, where do I get that for him? There's no way he's ready to go find himself a meal like Deidre or I can. Do I drag someone home for him?

"Don't borrow trouble," Deidre advises. "One thing at a time, Silas. You know how this works. You're usually the logical one."

I force myself to breathe, which only gives me a mouthful of Theo's changing scent. He still smells like himself, but all the human aspects are fading. Like all vampires, he smells colder now. His blood, his body, his life—it'll all be steeped in death now.

"I'll give him blood," a voice behind us says. I whirl to see my father standing there, dressed in a robe and slippers. I've never seen this man at anything less than his best before. But he's out here in slippers, looking at us on the ground.

"What?" I croak.

He kneels in the dirt next to us. "You chose him over everything, and I can respect that. As you reminded me, the mating bond is sacred. If he's what you need, then I'll make sure you have him."

He looks at Theo for a long moment, sitting in the dirt and just watching instead of doing anything. Deidre keeps feeding Theo her blood, and something goes soft in my father's eyes.

I don't even know his true mate's name. He never speaks of her, but I can see the memory of her in his eyes right now, and I feel softer toward him than I have in decades. Theo will survive tonight. He'll be changed, but he'll live. And I don't know who I'd be if that wasn't true.

In one sharp moment, he bites his wrist open and gently pushes Deidre out of the way, replacing her arm with his own. "Almost done, son," he murmurs to me. I stroke Theo's hair. I can feel it too; he's changing.

My father pulls back long before Deidre or I did, but Theo is stirring in our shared grip. "That's it, darling," I murmur. "You're fine. Come back to me, now."

"Give him some time," Deidre says, but I can feel that Theo doesn't need time. He's already fighting his way back to me.

"Get him inside," my father suggests. "He doesn't need to wake up in the dirt."

He's right, so I carefully take Theo in my arms and carry him back to the house. I ignore everything on the way to our bedroom. I'm sure there's a mess to clean up, but that sounds like a problem for another day. Only one thing matters now.

When we're in our room, I strip all of our clothes off, wanting to get the bloody, filthy clothes away from us. I'll call for a bath once he's awake, but for now it's enough that we're skin to skin like this, huddled in our bed.

I press a kiss to his temple, then leave my mouth pressed there. "C'mon, love," I whisper. "I need you to wake up for me. I promise it'll all be okay, Theo. I'm here. You're safe; we all are."

I repeat similar messages for what feels like days, but is probably an hour at most. Then Theo's eyelids flutter, and I hold my breath until he's looking at me.

"Hello, darling," I whisper, and my heart stops when he smiles.

Chapter Twenty-One

Theo

My body feels oddly quiet. I was never aware that my body made noise, that every process and piece was so loud, but now, in the absence of all of it, the silence is deafening.

I'm quiet, but everything else is loud now. I can hear Silas' blood pumping, and the vague sounds of conversations downstairs. I can hear the old house settling and every breath Silas takes sounds like thunder.

"I'm changed?" I ask. My voice sounds different now, too. Something about it is deeper, more resonant.

Silas' arms tighten around me. "What do you remember?"

"Everything." I remember the attack, and using the weapon I made to protect myself from the king. I remember Silas and Deidre and even their father saving me.

"You're changed," Silas confirms, voice heavy. "I'm sorry if that's not what you wanted."

"I wanted forever with you," I tell him. And if I wanted it as a human, it's nothing on what I want right now. I feel what Silas always meant when he talked about the mating bond. Silas is in my bones, something I need to live as much as blood, as much as air. He is me and I am him. We can never exist alone and be everything we're meant to be.

I tasted three different people's blood tonight, but I can pick out Silas' immediately. The flavor still lingers on my tongue, sweet and filling. I was dying, and I still knew. He's my mate.

He's been holding me, but I suddenly need to hold him back. I need to tie him to me in a way that he can't escape, because I need him to survive now. I sit up and grab at his arms, pressing his hold on me tighter so neither of us can escape this.

"Well, we have forever," Silas says, kissing the side of my neck. It's where my wound should be, I realize belatedly, but I don't feel any pain. I risk letting go of Silas long enough to touch that spot, and only feel clean, unbroken skin.

"Healed?"

"While you were changing. No more injuries for you."

No more. Rowan will never beat me bloody again because I'll just heal from it. No more cuts and scrapes and no more pain. I'm immortal.

I'm immortal. I can't quite wrap my mind around that yet.

But I do know it means I get to keep Silas forever. I know it means that we can build that future we barely dared to begin to dream about.

And suddenly, the quiet in my body is interrupted by a pain like I'm starving. My stomach curls and my body aches for something so hard that my limbs shake.

"Theo?"

"I—fuck, I don't know, I—" Did we somehow mess up vampirism? Could my body reject the change?

"You're hungry," Silas says, his voice carefully even despite the fact that I can hear him barely hiding his panic. "You need blood."

"You just gave me so much blood," I protest through gritted teeth. It had taken three vampires bleeding themselves nearly dry for me to change. I can't already need more blood.

"I told you, vampiric blood isn't good enough—we've already cycled through all the nutrients in the blood. It changed you but it won't feed you. I need to get more for you." His arms tighten around me.

"Where?" I never asked him where he goes for blood. He told me he doesn't usually kill people, but not where. Can I even get there? Will my body know what to do?

There's a knock on the door, and Silas holds me tighter. "Come in." He pulls the blanket tighter around us, and it's only then I realize I'm naked.

I almost protest, because I don't want anyone to see me like this, but it's Deidre with a cup in hand. "Margueritte organized a little donation for you," she says after looking me over. "She worries."

"Her blood?" I croak, touched by the thought.

Deidre shrugs. "And Joseph's and Michael's. They offered more if you need it. You shouldn't, but who knows how much healing all that took out of you?"

"Donated?" I ask skeptically.

"They insisted."

"They don't even know me." Why would anyone do that for me?

"No," Deidre agrees. "But they know him. They like Silas. Seem to think he's a fair lord of the house and want to make you welcome here, since you make him happy."

Silas' arms tighten around me. "Thank them for me, will you?" he asks, voice choked up. He kisses the side of my head again. "And when you're better, I'll show you how to go about feeding yourself."

I wrinkle my nose. "I didn't think about actually drinking blood."

"I don't know many turned vampires, but I think it'll be as instinctive to you as it is to us," Deidre promises me. "Try it."

I take the proffered cup with reservations, but Deidre is right. As soon as the blood is in my sight, my body knows what to do.

My fangs—and it's only now that I realize I have fangs—feel overly sensitive, despite the fact that I don't need to bite anything to take in my meal. The blood is soothing on my throat, some life-giving nectar that I greedily gulp down.

Silas holds me the entire time. I think that helps me keep an open mind about this.

I feel stronger the second I finish drinking. The pain eases, and my senses are somehow even sharper than they were when I woke up. I turn to look at Silas. He's watching me with weary eyes, but as soon as we make eye-contact he breaks out into a grin. I can see every pore of his skin, every hair, every beloved inch of him.

Deidre takes the cup from my slack fingers. "I'll take care of everything here," she promises us. "You take all the time you need."

"Thank you," I manage, but I can't stop looking at Silas.

I hear the door click shut behind her as she leaves, and Silas must take that as our cue, because he pushes me gently onto the bed and kisses me slowly. He licks into my mouth, no doubt tasting every drop of blood I just drank.

"Forever," he promises against my lips, and I kiss him back in response. Forever. So many promises in that one word.

He presses lighter kisses to my lips, then my jaw. "I'll teach you how to hunt," he promises. "Keep you fed."

I wrinkle my nose. "I have to feed from other people? Can't I just feed from you?" I think I can tolerate feeding from him. If it's anything like when he fed from me, then I think I'll enjoy it thoroughly. But drinking from other people just sounds unclean.

Silas tilts his neck like just the thought of it makes him excited. "You can drink from me whenever you want," he promises. "Unfortunately for you, my blood is used up and not very good for you. You need real food, Theo. It won't be that bad."

If he says so. I admit the blood I just drank felt like the elixir of life, but the idea of puncturing someone's skin to drink from them still sends unpleasant shivers down my spine.

I wrinkle my nose at the thought, but set it aside for now. "Can I drink from you right now?" I ask.

Silas' pupils blow wide, and he nods rapidly. His mouth falls open, and I see his chest rise and fall with little panting breaths.

Oh, he likes that idea. I run an experimental tongue over my left fang, wondering how it'll feel to pierce his skin with it. The idea of biting him is infinitely more appealing than biting some random stranger.

"Are you ready for that?" Silas asks. "You don't have to be. You almost died tonight."

"But I didn't die. And now I'm going to live forever."

"Exactly, forever. We have forever to try this; it doesn't have to be tonight."

"Do you not want to fuck me, Silas?"

His breath catches for a moment. "I'll fuck you any place, any time, darling," he murmurs. "Just as long as it's what you want."

"I want." I shift so I'm straddling him, pressing my hands into his chest so he stays flat on the bed. Even my hands are more sensitive than they were before. I feel a million pinpricks with his skin against mine. I twitch my hand, but the feeling isn't unpleasant. It's like I can't help but feel him, like my focus is absorbed by him.

"You'll have to let me up, darling. Unless you plan on just falling on me and feasting."

"Not a bad idea," I murmur, exploring his chest with my fingers, then trailing down his sides to his sharp hip bones. "Would you let me?"

"Darling, I'd let you drain me dry. Take what you want."

I let my lips follow the trail my fingers left. Silas seems to be holding stone-still beneath me, waiting for me to make a decision.

I suck his cock into my mouth. He groans, long and low, letting his head fall back. I'm paranoid about my new fangs, but he was right when he told me it's not that difficult to negotiate them.

"Darling," he pants, "You can suck me all day, but if you anticipate anything else, it'll have to be now."

I swirl my tongue around the tip, tasting the bead of pre-come that lends credibility to his claim. When his thigh muscles tense, I back off, giving him a second to breathe while I contemplate what I want next.

"Sit up for me?" I ask him.

He scrambles to sit against the headboard, and I slide onto his lap. Silas' hands find my hips, thumbs stroking over the skin there. "Do you want to ride me, darling?"

"I'm going to ride you," I confirm. "And when I'm ready, I'm going to bite you."

"Fuck me," he hisses, trying to reach for the drawer he keeps the oil in without dislodging me. I move enough for him to reach, then settle back into my spot as soon as I can. He uncorks the bottle, then slicks his fingers and slides two inside me.

I grind back onto his fingers, letting them stretch me and leaning into the feeling. Every time he touches me I feel like I'm on fire, and I can't help but chase more of it.

"Enough," I rasp. "Enough, I need—I need—"

Silas searches out my mouth and pulls me into a kiss. "I know exactly what you need," he promises, and it's only once he says it that I realize he pulled his fingers out of me. I'd protest, but he fills me with his cock, so deep and easy it makes me throw my head back.

"Fuck." It barely comes out at all, the words swallowed by the immense pleasure I feel. Silas fills me right up, and I rotate my hips, looking for the perfect angle. I find it quick enough, and I see stars.

"That's it," Silas encourages, his voice a broken rasp as he watches me move against him. "You're so perfect, darling, so perfect, fuck yourself on me, take your pleasure—"

I'm not going to last much longer, and Silas seems to know it, grabbing my chin and forcing me to look at him. I grind my hips, unable to really move with him holding me, but even the little circling motions I can make are driving me higher and higher.

"Listen to me, darling," Silas says firmly. "When you come, I want you to bite me."

It takes me a moment to understand what he said. "What if I hurt you?" I have no idea how to do this without hurting him.

He tightens his grip on my chin and pulls me in for a kiss. "You won't hurt me," he promises. "Bite me, Theo. I want your mark more than anything."

He hisses when I clench around him at just the thought. He wants my mark on him. He wants me to bite him.

Fuck me. I'm so close, and before I can overthink it, I lean down to suck and kiss his neck, getting ready to bite him.

Silas' hand unexpectedly wraps around my cock, and I'm done for. I have just enough presence of mind to sink my teeth into his skin as the pleasure overwhelms me.

Fuck, I've never tasted anything sweeter. Some part of me understands what Silas meant about this blood being more like a dessert than a meal—it doesn't feel very substantial, but it's damn sweet. But mostly, I'm just consumed in the earth-shattering, toe-curling ecstasy of how much of my mate I get right now.

And when he comes, shouting my name and shooting his come inside me, it somehow tastes even sweeter.

CHAPTER TWENTY-TWO

SILAS

Despite me being the one who literally had his blood sucked, I'm the one with a half-collapsed mate on top of me who I need to coax into moving.

I can't really blame him. Between his new immortality and the sensory overload that comes with that, and the sheer number of sensations we just subjected him to, anyone would pass out.

"How do you feel?" I murmur, pushing sweaty hair off his forehead.

He grins at me, his smile looking drugged and blissful. "So good."

I kiss that sweaty forehead. "That's good." I move to stand, looking for something to clean us up with, but Theo catches my wrist.

I turn to look at him when he doesn't let go. "There's never been anything as good as you," he says to me, voice serious now. His thumb strokes the bones of my wrist. "Just... needed you to know that."

I mentally add the fact that he's dealing with the discovery of what a mating bond feels like on top of all the other sensations, but it doesn't make my heart flutter any less. "I love you, too," I tell him, turning my wrist so I can slide from his grip and hold his hand instead. "Beyond measure, beyond words. Forever." I hesitate for a moment. "Could you see a future? Here? With me?"

His brow furrows, and I have a brief moment of panic before he says, "Of course. Always. But I thought your father was going to make you leave?"

I grin. "I have a solution for that," I tell him. "But that's tomorrow's problem. So, assume I'm staying. Would you be happy here? I won't be my father's heir. Just a vampire with a lot of land and a lot of books."

Theo snorts. "Just," he mumbles derisively, and okay, I see his point. My life might not be what most royalty aspire to, but it is pretty grand when compared to what he used to know. "I think I'll manage."

Life might be complicated for the next little while. I have to get my father to accept the offer I want to make him, a tough offer for an old king who is too used to underestimating his children. And I suppose there's nothing to say that the coup attempt is officially over, although I hope to move any future attempts away from my home. And in addition to all that, I have a young mate who needs to learn what it means to be a vampire. As much as I liked him drinking from me, he can't do that all the time. Nor will my household staff be content to always drip their own blood into a cup. He needs to learn how to properly feed himself.

A lot to do. But none of it has to start right now, and none of it has to get in the way of this moment.

I settle for the edge of the sheet, knowing it'll need to be washed in the evening regardless, and clean the two of us up, including dabbing blood from the corner of Theo's mouth. Then I slide into bed with him, pulling him close, and bury my face in his neck so we can sleep.

***

By the time we wake up, it's well after sunset. Theo seems especially groggy, and I fight down concern. It's probably normal, given everything he just went through, although I don't know enough made vampires to be sure. I resolve to keep a close eye on him, but the truth is the best thing I can do is probably to get him up and moving and adapted to his new life.

Besides, there's something happening today that I want him to see.

The whole house has been cleaned. There's no sign of Donatella's death, and if I went to the garden, I'd wager that Isaac is gone, too. Someone took care of it all, protecting the sanctity of our home. Deidre, I imagine. She's exactly the type of person to take care of details like that.

Which means she's exactly the type of person who's perfect for what I spoke to my father about before all this nonsense. He's underestimated his daughters for too long. But I think the sheer number of sons who failed him recently have perhaps opened his eyes.

Deidre is, as expected, in the library. She looks up when we walk in and smiles. "We didn't want to leave until we could speak with you."

"Leave?" Theo asks, stopping just behind me.

"He didn't tell you?" She sets her book aside and stands, graceful as ever. "No, I suppose you two have been busy." She walks closer, coming to a stop just in front of us and looking at Theo. "I'm going with our father."

"Why?" He blurts it out like he couldn't fathom wanting to do it.

She shrugs. "He had a change of heart about who he wanted there. I'm sure Silas here had something to do with that." I open my mouth to protest, but she doesn't let me speak. "In the light of two attempts on his life, all from people close to him—a spy wouldn't be amiss."

"A crown princess who can get people to spill their secrets wouldn't be either," I murmur.

Deidre smiles mysteriously. "Now that would be telling."

Theo squeezes my hand, understanding now.

"You'll be careful," I tell her.

"I'd say I always am, but we'd both know that would be a lie," she says breezily.

Considering this whole thing started with her poisoning herself inadvertently, yes, we do. I swallow. "Try. For me."

She leans in and kisses my cheek. "You're still my favorite brother. And this is my favorite place. Don't think you'll get out of seeing me again. I'll be back." She steps back and picks up the book she was reading. "I'm taking this. I'll return it next time I visit."

"You better," I say, managing to sound menacing enough about the book when we all know full well that I only care about her visit.

She smiles. "I'll go tell him we're leaving. I have traitors to sniff out, and I don't want to waste time."

She flounces out of the library, leaving us in her wake. I have a feeling this is a portent of the rest of our lives with Deidre.

Theo squeezes my hand again. "You gave up being the crown prince for her."

I snort. "Let's not pretend it was a sacrifice. I'm more than happy here with my books." I let go of his hand so I can pull him into a proper embrace. "And my mate."

"And your mate," he agrees, holding the arms I have wrapped around him.

***

My father and Deidre leave that night. I make a half-hearted protest that they should wait another day, leave right at sunset tomorrow, but they're insistent and it's probably good. I want my father gone, and if I don't let Deidre leave now, then I might make a fool out of myself.

We watch until their carriage is out of sight, standing in the garden that Theo nearly died in. He doesn't seem leery of it, at least, which is good.

"I was thinking," he murmurs once my sister is long gone.

"Hm?"

"I told you once, after your father left, I wanted to bring Marielle here."

That is not where I thought he was going with that. I thought we were going to take advantage of having the house to ourselves. Perhaps we could finally fuck in the library without worrying about scandalizing Deidre.

But he's still focused on that little druid.

She must be something special.

I heave a sigh. "Alright, then," I agree. "I was just thinking this house was devoid of little sisters, anyways."

EPILOGUE: THEO

MODERN DAY

We didn't find Marielle on that trip. Silas and I decided I should learn to be a proper vampire before going to get her, and by the time I'd been able to manage my needs and drink without making a mess, the manor I'd been a prisoner in had been deserted.

It'd been hard to go back there, but it'd been harder still to find it empty. If I could still throw up, I'm sure I would have.

Silas promised to keep an ear to the ground. Deidre had promised to find out what she could, a much more promising proposition despite her increasing duties with her father. But we'd never turned anything up.

Until tonight.

Tonight, Marielle walked into our home on the arms of some giant werewolf, looking like a queen.

She's all grown up now. All the childish pieces of her are gone, and it sounds like they were ripped away from her a long time ago.

She leaves the party early, and I don't last much longer. It's rude for hosts to bail early, especially when the actual guest of honor isn't here yet—Deidre is, as always, fashionably late—but I don't really care tonight.

Silas follows me straight into the library, still a sanctuary for the both of us, even after all this time. "What's wrong, darling?"

I take off the ostentatious crown he always insists I wear. I know why he does it—vampires like his father, who have little respect for made vampires and even less for former humans, sometimes need to be reminded of their place and that I am a prince-consort of the realm—but it's heavy and obnoxious, and I prefer the days we sit around in comfortable clothes and read books.

But not tonight. Tonight I can't even think of relaxing and begin to pace.

Silas, as always, catches me. "She's here. That's a win, Theo."

"We left her there." The words rip out of me, sharp and painful, but they're true. We left her there, and we went back too late.

Silas squeezes me. "You did everything you could. You took care of yourself first. You prioritized her safety. And nothing that happened is your fault. She doesn't blame you, either."

No, she doesn't. I think her mate does, and I don't entirely blame him. And I usually wouldn't value some werewolf's opinion over Marielle's, but, well, I think she's wrong here.

She's been wronged by so many people, and I might not be the worst, but I'll put myself on that list.

Silas isn't having it, though. He grips my chin and tilts my head up so I'm forced to look at him. "She is here to try again. She doesn't blame you for what happened, and you shouldn't either. If you don't blame her for what happened to you, then accept that she doesn't blame you for what happened to her." I open my mouth to protest that it's different, but Silas doesn't give me a chance. "And if you want a chance to move forward with her, then you have to let it go."

That stops me short. He's right. Silas is always right about things like this, and I force myself to relax. "She seems happy," I murmur.

"I thought so too."

"She said she'd come back."

"Then you'll see her again. Preferably when we don't have half the known world here for Deidre to pry secrets out of," he grumbles.

I can't help but grin. Silas has done a good job all night at projecting the image of the confident, in-charge lavish prince who loves events like this, but I know we'll spend the next three days in bed with a stack of books and each other.

"We need to go back out there," I say after a moment, reluctantly turning my head to break his hold on my chin.

He's not having it. He pinches my chin again and tilts my head for a kiss, hot and demanding and making me lean into him to stay upright. My hands fight their place on his chest, using him to support me.

"Crown on, darling," he murmurs against my lips. "We have a party to dazzle."

So, with some part of me lighter than it's been in two centuries, I rejoin the party.

ABOUT THE AUTHOR

Addison James is a romance book author from New England. They are obsessed with all things mythical, mystical, and magical. A lifelong fantasy reader, that evolved to fantasy romance as they grew up. Addison always has a story to tell and is excited to introduce you to their world of fantasy romance. Addison can be reached through Tiktok, Instagram, or Threads (@Addyjameswriter), through email at addyjames@addyjameswriter.com, or through their website, www.addyjameswriter.com.